ANGEL OF MERCY

BOOK 1 - THE ANGEL OF MERCY SERIES

BRUCE LEWIS

Cover design: Tatiana Villa, https://www.viladesign.net/

Dedication

For Gerry, always by my side, looking into the future.

Special Thanks

Chris Patchell, USA Today best-selling and award-winning author, for her friendship, generosity, and publishing wisdom.

Check out her mystery novels at https://www.chrispatchell.com/

FOREWORD

"If you don't have liberty and self-determination, you've got nothing; that's what this country is built on ... And the ultimate self-determination is when you determine how and when you're going to die ..." —Jack Kevorkian, M.D., the 'Doctor of Death'

1

Veterinary surgeons Jim Briggs and Jenny Morrison finished stitching the soft white belly of their tiny patient, splinting her leg, and bandaging her head. After three hours of emergency surgery, they stepped back from the operating table, looked down at the light brown creature with big round eyes and a short snout, and sighed with relief.

"She's so small," said Briggs. "She weighed 2.5 ounces at birth. At five weeks, she's still only a pound."

"Jimmy, I think she'll be okay." Given the severity of the injuries, they knew her chances of survival were fifty-fifty.

"I hope so," he said, grimacing as he gazed at the wounded Chihuahua puppy.

"She's so damn cute," said Briggs. "And fragile. They can be fierce when they're adults, as small as they are. God help any big dog that gets in their face."

Their patient was Bella, the runt of a litter they had rescued a month before. A Gold Coast couple rushed her mother, Sofie, to PawsCare Emergency Hospital when they realized she was losing her battle to push out eight puppies

—not a world record, but much more than average. Bella and her seven siblings survived the birthing trauma and left the hospital healthy a few days later.

Bella's injuries resulted from the couple's three-year-old daughter kicking playfully at the puppy, who was scampering with her litter mates in the backyard. The impact sent the little dog four feet headfirst into a cinderblock wall.

"You warn kids to be careful with puppies, and they still get hurt," said Jenny. "What would we do if our kids did something like that?"

"Kids will be kids," he said, his eyes fixed on Bella, her chest rising and falling, intermittent yaps coming from her mouth as if dreaming.

"You'll be no help raising ours. I'll be the mean mother who metes out punishment, and you'll be the happy dad who soothes their delicate egos."

"Sounds about right," he said.

Having children was the elephant in the room. They had been together for six years and wanted to marry and have a family. Despite their professed love, an invisible barrier, like a force field, kept them from closing the gap.

Briggs was determined to return to Portland, Oregon, to open a mobile dog care service. Jenny said she needed to stay in Chicago, close to aging parents. Neither could think of a way to break the stalemate.

Cupping Bella's head—thin as an eggshell—Briggs slowly lifted and gently handed her to Jenny.

Tears slid down Briggs' cheeks. He was happy and sad at the same time—drained from the effort and relieved the little dog had survived the surgery.

Jenny wrapped the puppy in a blanket and placed her in a crate to confine her movements. They didn't want her to wake up, start bouncing around, and hurt herself.

Since joining PawsCare, Briggs had saved countless dogs; each was a victory, and all of them made him tear up. All were connected to the death of his first dog, Mac, a Beagle.

After a car struck and severely injured the hound, the local vet said euthanasia was best for everyone. It wasn't best for 12-year-old Briggs, who grieved for months. After witnessing Mac's death, Briggs decided veterinary medicine would be his life's work. He vowed never to let another dog die. It wasn't a promise he could keep.

"Briggs, you need to buck up," said Jenny. "Go to Windy City for a workout. I'll go home and read."

Windy City Boxing, Chicago's oldest boxing club, was Brigg's relief valve, a place to pound away the pain in his soul from the frequent life-and-death procedures he performed on canines.

Ten years had passed since he was an NCAA national boxing finalist, but he could still hold his own with the up-and-comers. Often, he taught them lessons in boxing basics and humility. And, on occasion, he got knocked on his ass.

Either way, he needed the transition between veterinarian and angel of mercy.

2

Awave of warm air swept across Lake Michigan before slathering a thick layer of fog over large swaths of the city. The creeping mist hid the detritus of a homeless encampment nestling the shore.

Homelessness is a plague everywhere. It is a pandemic in big cities like Chicago, not something a mask could tame. It's more like The Blob, from the 1950s horror movie, about an alien that appears as a living ball of tar, oozing out of the movie theater projection room onto an unsuspecting audience. Or rolling down the street, absorbing every living thing in sight.

There is no vaccine for homelessness. No easy exit for its victims. Except for a humane death.

Jim Briggs felt like Jack the Ripper, a phantasm—only the shadow of his six-foot-six mass visible as he crept toward his next homeless victims: Chicago Symphony Orchestra's former concertmaster Franklin Elton and tech billionaire Robert "Rob" Merritt III.

Before the accident, Elton was the Tom Brady of violinists. He dazzled audiences worldwide with his performances. He was a magician with the instrument. Observers were mystified at how a 6-foot-4-inch man, with hands the size of mountain lion paws, could produce such rich sounds with what appeared to be a toy under his massive chin.

Beautiful violin music, like Elton's, was described as having tonal colors, from bright and crisp to warm and mellow, with a range of dynamics "from the softest pianissimo to the loudest fortissimo." The descriptions were a foreign language to all but musicians and fans of classical music.

At his peak, he held his own with Nicola Benedetti and Joshua Bell, two of the world's greatest. Now, he was fingerless and homeless, living in a tent—a broken man. And Jim Briggs was coming to save him.

Squeaky leather sandals signaled Briggs' progress. For some, the sound passing their tent homes was soothing. The walker, they knew, was a benevolent man who cared deeply about their wellbeing. 'Dr. Jim' would be there to care for their dogs. He doctored them, too: sewing up a stab wound or cleaning and bandaging a cut or a head injury. They also knew, with absolute certainty, that when the killing streets of Chicago became unbearable, Dr. Jim—alias, the Angel of Mercy—would set them free.

Briggs was a football field away from his first stop as he strolled among the sick and forgotten. He took in the familiar grunts, groans, epithets, shouts, laughs, and barking dogs that often greeted his passing. They were the sounds of the godforsaken: the veterans suffering from PTSD, working families too poor to afford rent, the mentally ill who refused to take their medication, the addicts living in an altered universe, and those who no longer cared whether they lived or died.

Many of Chicago's houseless citizens loved the freedom

of the streets, as ugly and hostile as they could be. Some said they would rather die, carried out feet-first than hunker down on a steel cot in a crowded shelter, also known as a Navigation Center—to them, a synonym for prison.

Among those resigned to live their final days among the free was Rob Merritt. He was in line for a gentle exit from the world, just ahead of Frank Elton. Briggs had never killed two people on the same day. "There's a first time for everything, he said, looking at Molly, his golden retriever. She pawed his leg.

Merritt, 52, would be Briggs' 11th victim; Elton would make a dozen.

The first ten weren't exactly victims since they had begged to die. Still, raising the death toll to 12 weighed heavily on Briggs' mind and body. His 220 pounds felt like 500. He had tried his best to find alternatives for those he had sent to their death. In the end, he gave them what they wanted. He often felt like a one-man Make-A-Wish Foundation.

Occasionally, Briggs discovered an affordable home for an unsheltered family, got a meth addict into treatment, or found permanent housing for a veteran. While he had delivered a two-shot death cocktail of the anesthetic Propofol and phenobarbital nearly a dozen times, he had turned down another 30 requests. He had no system for evaluating who should live or die. His brain played a game of heads or tails. Heads, a yea, was a punch in the gut. So, why do it?

Blame his father, James Allen Briggs Sr. His dad, a newspaper crime reporter, was a devotee of Jack Kevorkian, known as Dr. Death. Kevorkian championed the right to die by physician-assisted suicide, telling the press and the world, "Dying is not a crime."

After Dr. Death was convicted of second-degree murder

and sentenced to 10 to 25 years in prison, Briggs' father joined a secret army of people who shared Kevorkian's vision. They called themselves Jack's Angels. His dad had taken him on two assisted suicides. In each case, Briggs had been shocked at the patient's pain, the lack of help from their doctors, and the terrible end they faced without help: a long, torturous downward spiral. The young Briggs felt satisfied knowing he had helped relieve their suffering.

Briggs stopped momentarily, closed his eyes, took a deep breath, and listened to the cacophony of city sounds, then walked on. Standing outside Rob Merritt's tent, covered by a faded red rain tarp, he recalled his conversations with the dying man. Merritt had shared a tattered family album with Briggs in making his case for a peaceful death.

Photos showed a tall, broad-shouldered man with a square jaw and cleft chin. Bright blue eyes under thick black hair and eyebrows that radiated energy and hope. A later photo from Merritt's days as CEO of a tech start-up showed him at his full height, with a broad grin, his hat cocked just so. Like a fedora, the hat resembled Frank Sinatra's signature Trilby but with a slightly narrower brim. A classic. A fabulous look then. Still cool for artists and the super-rich.

A newspaper clipping claimed Merritt had sold his company for $5 billion. Unfortunately, his post-CEO life was like a shooting star that burns up when it hits the atmosphere.

That same successful man was now pleading for Briggs to kill him. How Merritt had arrived at the end of his road was an all too familiar story among the homeless. Merritt's 10-year-old daughter, an only child, had died in a bicycle accident. He and his wife couldn't cope. They blamed each other. Divorce followed.

After the divorce, Merritt spiraled downward like a

pheasant hit with a shotgun blast. He quit going to parties and avoided the social circles that had made him famous. A decade of alcoholism followed, resulting in cirrhosis, liver cancer, and a dwindling number of sunsets. Merritt wanted a gentle but swift exit. Money meant nothing to him. Since losing his daughter, he hadn't touched a cent of his wealth, blaming his inattention to his daughter for her tragic accident. He was inconsolable.

Still, Briggs wondered if someone from Merritt's orbit would come to his rescue. Or if a hospice program would ease him into his final days. Briggs' girlfriend, Jenny Morrison, had researched Merritt's life, looking at social media and newspaper clippings detailing his professional accomplishments. She learned his ex-wife had married a prominent doctor and was living in Southern California. How hard would it be to get Merritt into a medical treatment program and back on his feet? The odds were long. Still, there was hope.

Briggs called out just loud enough to pierce the paper-thin walls of Merritt's dome tent. A zipper slid down, and a greasy head of hair poked out.

He reached out and shook Briggs' hand. "Dr. Jim, please come in." The man was polite and welcoming. He held Briggs' hand until he was inside, afraid to lose a grip on his savior. There was gratefulness in his shaky voice. Molly stood guard outside.

For the next half hour, like a defense attorney pleading with a jury to spare the death penalty, Briggs offered Merritt the possibility of redemption, a cancer treatment, and lots of sunrises.

"God bless you," said Merritt. "Always the optimist, aren't you? Every living thing has a sell-by date: a beginning and an end. I'm ready to embrace that end wherever it may take me."

Briggs recognized determination in the man's rheumy eyes. They were focused, unblinking. His sallow skin hung from his puffy face. The explosion of red veins on his nose confirmed the depth of his alcoholism. His ragged clothes further attested to Merritt's decline.

"You're sure?"

Merritt smiled weakly and nodded.

3

Jim Briggs had killed ten homeless people with animal euthanasia drugs—drugs that American veterinarians use to humanely put down a million dogs a year. The old, sick, and unadoptable dogs—many strays—must make way for new inmates to fill the so-called no-kill shelters. They had no say over their destiny.

By contrast, Chicago's 4,500 unsheltered human strays could decide for themselves, choosing death over a life that wouldn't end well.

Rob Merritt, a depressed billionaire with liver cancer, a failed marriage, and the tragic loss of his only child, wanted to exit the mean streets of Chicago. He said he felt like one of those shelter animals destined to die.

Briggs had given Merritt a day to think about which path he wanted to follow: one with a cancer cure and a future or death. Now he was back, sitting in the man's tent, waiting for an answer.

"Rob, are you okay?"

Recovering from his thousand-yard stare, Merritt smiled at Briggs and said he was ready.

Briggs smiled back, opened his medical bag, and pulled out a syringe and two vials. How many times had he performed the death ritual? After a decade of caring for dogs, he had lost track. He was conflicted despite standing as a foot soldier in the Kevorkian Army. Was killing a human murder, or was it assisted suicide?

Nine states and the District of Columbia allow physician-assisted suicide. Illinois wasn't one of them. And Briggs was not a physician. With no capital punishment, life imprisonment was assured.

He couldn't claim he was assisting suicides with the hope of a lighter sentence since he injected the death cocktail directly into his homeless clients.

The cops, the prosecutor, and the jury would agree it was murder. Perhaps not first-degree, but murder, just the same.

Besides, Merritt was ready to die. He had confirmed it several times. So, how could Briggs say no?

"Why do you do this?" Merritt asked as Briggs filled the first syringe with Propofol, the anesthetic that would render the homeless man unconscious. It would prevent him from feeling the heart-stopping, lung-suffocating pain of the barbiturate to follow.

Briggs put down the syringe, closed his eyes, and smoothed his long red hair behind his ears, tightening the rubber band on his ponytail. He tugged on his thick red beard like a scholar pondering a mystery.

"When I was a boy, we had to put down my dog," said Briggs. "He was hurt, sick, and needed relief. The decision to end his life was one of the hardest I ever made. My mother told me it was mine to make—a life lesson. Afterward, I cried. I mourned that dog for months. But in my heart, I knew I had done the right thing. He needed me to speak for him. He deserved a dignified end, and I gave it to him. Good people like you, who have been dealt a shitty hand, deserve to choose how you get to live and die. I'm standing up for your right to make that choice." He didn't mention Jack Kevorkian. The sad pet story was motivation enough, he thought.

"I get it," said Merritt. "Thank you."

"Do you have time for one more story before you go?" Briggs said as if Merritt was about to head to the gym or a business appointment.

"Sure," he said, laughing and shaking his head like it was the funniest thing he had ever heard.

Was Briggs stalling? Maybe, which is why he launched into the story of Frank Elton, former concertmaster of the Chicago Symphony Orchestra—another homeless man who wanted to die.

"Elton wowed audiences worldwide with his virtuoso violin performances before he lost three fingers in an accident," Briggs said. His phone lit up a minute into his story.

He held up a finger to Merritt.

"Hi Jen, what's up? Is Bella okay?

"Don't obsess," she said. "That puppy is tough as they come. She's looking better every day. She's nearly out of the woods."

"Good news."

"Have you finished with Mr. Merritt?"

"Just about to start," said Briggs. "Why?"

"I got in touch with his ex-wife. It's good news."

"I'll be right there," he said.

"I've got an emergency at home," Briggs lied. "I know how important this is to you. I want your final moments to be relaxed and for you to feel at peace. I'll be back as soon as I can. Most likely, it will be at the same time tomorrow. Will you be okay until then?"

"Go," said Merritt. "I had a family once. I know how important it is to be there for them. I'm not going anywhere. At least until you return."

Briggs leaned forward, hugged the bedraggled man, put the syringe in his medical bag, and crawled out of the tent into the foggy night.

He took his time getting home since there was no emergency, stopping at another tent where a light was left outside —a sign that a person's dog needed help. A three-legged rescue mutt had gotten into a scrape with a German Shepherd mix and required stitches. When Briggs walked in the front door of his Gold Coast townhouse an hour later, he grabbed Jenny and hugged her.

"You're a lifesaver. Your timing was amazing. I was one minute away from killing the guy. Now I know how a prison warden feels, waiting for a call from the governor—hoping beyond hope—that the condemned will get a last-minute reprieve. Although you believe the condemned person's death will serve justice, you don't want to be the one delivering it. I feel that way more and more."

Tears trickled down Briggs' face.

Jenny, 6 feet tall, had to stand on her tiptoes to kiss Briggs, who was a half foot taller. She grabbed his beard and pulled him down to her. "It's okay. You're doing the right thing."

"Merritt's ex-wife, Peggy Garland, was horrified at his deteriorated condition," Jenny explained. "He had gone completely silent; she hadn't heard a peep from him in years and figured he was dead or hiding. The good news is that she is married to a doctor who works at a major teaching hospital in Southern California. They want to help. They'll pay all his expenses. Her husband can get him into one of the country's best cancer treatment programs offering the latest drug trials. Because of their money and status before Elton disappeared, he'll be in a luxury apartment near the medical center with full-time caregivers. It's a win-win."

Briggs took a deep breath. "It's a win-win if we can convince him he doesn't need to die."

4

Rob Merritt's death was on hold for the moment with his ex-wife, Peggy, offering to help him with his medical problems and his life. Merritt still was determined to die. However, he agreed first to consider her offer of free housing and the best cancer treatment at no cost to him. Not that he needed the money. He could walk into any bank, show his ID, withdraw any amount of money, and live in a $1,000-a-day hotel.

But Merritt e was depressed, slowly wasting away, and couldn't care less about money. Briggs had convinced him to get on the phone and talk to Peggy. Hearing her voice might re-create the connection they once felt.

A few days later, Briggs made the call and handed Merritt his phone. The conversation started slowly, with Merritt stuttering like a slipping bicycle chain, unable to lock into gear. He mostly listened, the range of emotions playing out on his face like a mime. After hanging up, he sobbed uncontrollably.

"I'm so damn confused. Peggy makes the alternative to death sound appealing. She always was an optimist, only dragged down by my self-centered obsession with my job and status, which left little time or attention for her or our daughter. I'm to blame for everything: the divorce, the public firestorm over my disappearance, and my daughter's death."

"Her death was an accident," Briggs said.

"Maybe so, but if I had been a better father who taught his daughter basic bike safety, she might be alive."

Briggs said nothing about the accident, changing the subject to Merritt's decision to live or die.

"Sleep on it," said Briggs. "I'll come by tomorrow evening."

AFTER A FULL DAY of patients and surgeries at Paws Care, the canine emergency hospital where he and Jenny were owner-partners, Briggs grabbed two slices of pizza and began his night shift. He would be up late offering his veterinary services for free to the residents of Lazy Acres.

The name had been written with a black marker pen on a piece of cardboard and nailed to a wood post next to Mattie Powell's tent home. She had chosen the name and insisted—tongue-in-cheek—she was the mayor.

Mayor Powell was a used-up addict, a skeleton of a woman with bad teeth and skin but a sweet disposition. Briggs was shocked when she showed him a picture of her a decade earlier. She had been a radiant blond, elegantly coiffed, with perfect teeth and bright blue eyes. It was hard for him to reconcile the picture with the woman before him. Her current state was a classic example of how life on the street killed the soul, then the individual.

Mattie claimed to have been a crime fiction author,

publishing a half dozen books before her husband cleaned out their bank accounts to pay gambling debts and ran off with another woman. Briggs had looked her up online, confirming the story. He downloaded one book and read it on his tablet. It was a damned good novel. So how did she go from a best-selling author to a human invisible to society? It was a short journey, according to her. And it wasn't pretty.

Mattie had discovered that her husband had been taking out big loans on their $2 million home, which had no mortgage. Left with nothing, she found herself on the street. That was five years ago. Now, she was on a downward trajectory. Briggs liked her. She had gathered life stories during her days as a prolific novelist and from her neighbors in the tent town of Lazy Acres. She had shared them, in stunning detail, during his frequent visits.

"Can't you live on book royalties? Briggs said.

"My contracts ran out long ago, and I never checked back with the publisher about renewing them. With no signed contract, the publisher had to pull the books from the market, and the money quickly dried up."

Briggs shook his head. A sad story.

"Jim, that was a lie. I'm sorry. I have plenty of money. I just can't face any more book deadlines or the public scrutiny that would come with the revelation that I had become a homeless drug addict."

"I get it," he said, feeling a stab at his heart. He adored Mattie Powell. She was a humanitarian, a tireless worker for everyone at Lazy Acres, paying little attention to her deteriorating health.

Besides her talent as a storyteller, Powell also was his referral source for neighbors with dogs who needed help and for her fellow travelers who were on life's final approach, ready to land.

"Mayor Powell, got a story for me today?"

"Yep." There was a gleam in her eyes, a smile crinkling her sun-spotted cheeks.

He waited.

"Wish I had a happy one. My little Sofi dog is ailing. Her stomach hurts. She's throwing up."

"Let me look."

The terrier knew Briggs and didn't object when he lifted her. Normally, she would lick his face when he brought her close. Not today.

"What's she been eating?"

Briggs knew his unsheltered clients could buy food in local markets with their panhandling collections. Dumpster-diving near fast-food restaurants and behind supermarkets supplemented their diet. They shared the meager pickings with their dogs.

Powell looked away. "Probably my fault. I got a $10 donation and bought a family-size bag of Cheetos. We ate the whole damn thing. One for her, then one for me." Briggs grimaced.

"Promise me you won't feed her any more Cheetos. Too much salt and whatever else they have. Not good for this little girl's tummy."

"You don't like Cheetos?"

"What's not to like?" said Briggs, smiling. "But not the best snack for a dog. You can give her one or two, but that's it. You promise?"

"I promise," Powell said sheepishly. Briggs knew she would share everything with Sofi despite his warning. Still, he had to try.

"Give her water but nothing else for the next twelve hours. Let her stomach settle. She'll be good as new after that."

"Hey, Doc, I got a nasty cut today climbing into a dumpster."

Briggs removed a rag covering a gash on her leg. After cleaning and bandaging the wound, he gave her a tetanus shot. Since veterinarians aren't licensed to administer shots to humans, Briggs had gotten a paramedic license to avoid legal problems. Ironic, given his angel of Mercy service. A local physician who ran a free clinic agreed to be his supervisor.

"Hey, big man, thanks for everything," said Powell.

"My pleasure."

"Before you go, tell me what's happening with Mr. Merritt."

"Looks like his ex-wife may rescue him."

"God bless America," she said.

"Rob still needs to decide if he wants help. He could expect a long, healthy life ahead if he accepts the deal. He would have a permanent home in Southern California."

"Maybe I should go kick his butt," said Powell. She lit a cigarette and started coughing. She touched her finger to her tongue, removed a bit of tobacco, and flicked it onto the grass.

"I think a little butt-kicking is just what the doctor ordered," Briggs said. She smiled and nodded.

Briggs knew Powell had COPD but said nothing. His mother was a lifelong smoker with burned-out lungs. Nicotine was as addicting as cocaine or heroin, he knew. Some experts said it was even more addicting. Lecturing his mother, or Powell, about the health risks of smoking was like putting a red flag in front of a bull. It just pissed them off. He avoided the subject, aware that she would likely request her own death soon enough. In the meantime, her compassion for the suffering of other homeless was enormous.

After finishing his unofficial "shift" doctoring the dogs of the homeless, Briggs walked home. Between his clinic hours, which included two emergency surgeries, and his evening with those experiencing the vagaries of homelessness, his workday had stretched to 12 hours.

Jenny, who had finished her clinic hours early, hugged him at the front door. She led him into the kitchen, handed him a beer, then patted the barstool. He sat down, took a long drink, and asked about her day.

"Compared with the three hours you spent in surgery repairing the leg of that Doberman hit by a car, I'd say mine was hunky-dory."

"What's for dinner?"

"Pasta Puttanesca."

"My favorite," he said.

"Jim, you can't kill Frank Elton," she blurted. The outburst jolted them.

Briggs sat up straight, took two gulps of his beer, and looked at her, waiting for more.

"I looked him up on YouTube. He's a musical genius. His violin playing is pure magic. I have little knowledge or interest in symphonies and symphony orchestras. But Elton's performances were incredible. His finger movements are so fast and subtle, like a magician, that you can't figure out where the sound comes from.

After dinner, Jenny showed Briggs a half dozen videos of Elton in concert and in a classroom, teaching.

"Wow," said Briggs.

"Look at these," said Jenny, handing him a printout of two Chicago Tribune articles describing the accident that killed Elton's career and robbed him of his identity and self-worth.

Frank Elton had been the concertmaster for the Chicago Symphony Orchestra for a decade.

That was before the gruesome accident that lopped off the tips of three fingers.

5
———

The event that changed Frank Elton's life and sent him into a death spiral was a story not unfamiliar to craftsmen and woodworkers everywhere. One slip of the saw, goodbye finger, or hand. Fellow musicians were shocked. None of them would go near a power tool, especially a band saw, like the one that permanently crippled their colleague.

According to news reports, Elton was in his garage, ears covered with sound-deadening headphones, listening to concert music while cutting wood for his five-year-old daughter's dollhouse. As he fed a piece of wood through his bandsaw, he saw something out of the corner of his eye. He looked up just as his daughter tried to pull herself up to watch him work. Just inches from cutting off her hand with the saw, he lunged at his daughter to protect her, shoving his hand into the saw. In a flash, three fingertips and Elton's future evaporated.

'Get mommy,' Elton had yelled to his terrified daughter as he grabbed for a shop towel and wrapped his hand. His next thought, he told the Tribune reporter, "was to find my fingers so I could get them sewn on. I wanted to finish the dollhouse." When asked about potential problems playing the violin with damaged fingers, he said, "They'll be good as new in no time, and I'll be back to work." It was a delusion, of course.

A team of specialists reattached the fingers during an eight-hour surgery. They declared the operation a success— to Elton's relief and to the relief of the entire orchestra. He waited for his hand to heal.

All was going well, feeling coming back into his fingers and the wounds healing when an infection set in. Two weeks later, the fingers were amputated to save his hand. It was a grim ending to a storybook career and the beginning of Elton's downward spiral into depression and alcoholism, and soon, death.

After reading the articles and watching the videos, Briggs headed for Elton's home—a two-man tent—to deliver the bad news: Briggs would not be his angel of mercy. Briggs had other ideas. The conversation wouldn't go well.

"Frank, it's Dr. Jim. Can I come in?"

"Thank God you're here," Elton said with a slur. "I can't stand the pain any longer,"

The two big men stuffed themselves into Elton's tent. They sat cross-legged, facing each other, their heads pushing up the top of the tent, their faces about a foot apart.

"Frank, I know the past few years have been a personal hell for you," Briggs said in a near whisper. "I watched YouTube videos, read articles about your performances worldwide, and news accounts of the accident."

"Yeah, well, what are you going to do?" said Elton, closing his eyes and rubbing his face. He reached down, picked up a flask, and pushed it toward Briggs.

"No, thank you," he said. "I've got a fresh growler of beer waiting for me at home."

"I know you want to end your pain, once and for all. I take your request seriously. However, you should know that assisting someone with suicide is a felony and a threat to my career. Helping you could put me in jail for life. On the other side of this coin, a flood of well-wishers started a GoFundMe campaign to raise money for your surgery and aftercare."

He held up his left hand. "You see these mutilated fingers?"

Briggs nodded.

"End of the story. Before these fingers were cut off, they thrilled concertgoers worldwide. They brought tears to people's eyes. They generated waves of standing ovations. Reviewers gushed at my virtuoso performances. I was treated like a god in music circles. Now, I can't use them to pick my nose. People around here laugh when I flip them off with my middle stub. I'm done with this humiliation, and I'm done with life. Dr. Jim, you're my ticket to ride— whether it's to Hell or someplace else. I don't care. I want to go—now."

"I'll need more than that," Briggs pushed back. "There's something you aren't telling me. As painful as it might be, you need to tell me the truth. We both have skin in this game. I've got to feel your pain."

Elton stared at him, his eyes slits, his jaws pulsing.

"Frank, I'm not a counselor. I don't have a degree in psychology or crisis intervention. However, I've staffed a suicide hotline. Your story is familiar. I've heard it hundreds of times. I have a few questions I need you to answer before I can take that final step with you."

Elton realized Briggs wasn't giving him the quick fix he wanted.

"Okay, shoot. What do you want to know?"

"The truth."

"I'm not sure you—or the world—can handle the truth."

6

J im Briggs had refused to kill former world-famous concert violinist Frank Elton until he got a few answers to some life-altering questions.

Briggs wasn't sure why, but his gut told him there was more to the story than a simple wood shop mishap. And now he was back in Elton's tent home to get some answers.

"The GoFundMe campaign raised a half million dollars to help pay your medical bills while you were recovering. So why is the money still sitting there two years later?"

"No way I was taking charity."

"How did you pay your bills?

"My base pay was more than $600,000 a year. Touring, teaching, recordings, and merchandise sales added another $250,000. My wife and I were savers. And we had paid off the mortgage. Unfortunately, I decided against disability or hand insurance. Our finances were okay until co-pays and specialty care out-of-pockets began washing away the foundation of our financial security. Still, I was determined not to take the money."

"Did you ever consider that the donations came from

people whose lives you enriched through your music? And that they wanted to give something back?"

"That's one way to look at it."

"You're still not telling me something?"

Elton appeared ready to crawl into a hole and die rather than confess. But Briggs wouldn't budge on his demand for more transparency.

"I can see you'll need more for me to get the final rest I'm craving. Let's skip what it takes to achieve world-class status. Assume you have reached the top because you've damn near achieved perfection. And you need to be perfect in every one of your 150 performances each year as a Chicago Symphony Orchestra member. That doesn't count other performances you give as a solo or a quartet. Think of it this way: the orchestra is 94 musician superstars. They are like the precision moving parts in a million-dollar racecar. A single misfire can blow an engine or ruin a concert."

Briggs looked at him, waiting for more.

"I'm no hero," said Elton. "My daughter didn't enter the wood shop and jump toward the saw. I didn't push her away, falling into the saw blade with my hand as reported."

"It was a lie?"

"After 40 years of effortlessly playing the violin without thinking, my fingers failed me. They began cramping in the middle of performances. From the audience's perspective, nothing was amiss. Other orchestra members caught the bits of errant sound, as did Bill Goodman, our conductor. At Bill's suggestion, I reluctantly visited a neurologist with expertise in music and the brain. He did a full workup, then gave me a diagnosis." Elton stopped, took a deep drink of whiskey, and asked Briggs if he wanted to hear more. Briggs nodded.

"The doctor diagnosed my condition as focal dystonia.

He described the condition as a kind of muscle cramp that can develop when the hand is overdoing something it's very good at. It can cause problems for anybody who is highly skilled and working under pressure—a big hazard for musicians, but also typists, dentists, and hairdressers."

"It's akin to the Yips," said Briggs, "the sudden unexplained loss of athletic skills. Broadcasters talk about it all the time when a football player—with a long string of perfect kicks— can no longer make a routine field goal. Or a top-rated golfer suddenly can't make putts—regularly missing two footers."

"Sounds low-class to say a world-famous musician has the Yips," Elton said. "But I guess we are like elite athletes."

"What's the cure?"

"You won't believe this. The neurologist recommended Botox injections." As soon as the words came out of Elton's mouth, he started laughing uncontrollably. Tears and snot poured down his face, his shoulders shook, and he rolled on his side, barely able to talk.

Finally, he straightened up and said, "I visualized having 'trout lips' and thought the lips would distract the audience from my playing." A second later, Briggs had joined Elton's laughing jag. No doubt the neighbors would be coming to find out what was so funny.

"Botox and hand therapy were the antidotes, the doctor said. He said it was a common problem—one I could overcome. Given some rest and a break from the pressure of achieving performance perfection, it would resolve itself. I didn't have time to rest. I had too many commitments. And, of course, I continued to have an increasing number of performance failures. I should have listened to him."

"With your career slipping away, why didn't you take off a few months?"

"I should have. Instead, I got drunk. My daughter wasn't there, but I was working on the dollhouse. I got up from the bench to get another piece of wood. I felt dizzy and started to fall. I grabbed my workbench with one hand, and the table saw bench with the other to steady myself. My hand slipped and pushed right into the blade. My fingers were gone in a flash."

"Sorry, Frank," said Briggs. "I don't know what else to say. I wish I could wave a magic wand and bring them back."

"And here I am, at death's door, all because I was vain and stupid." Elton then looked away, tears cutting lines in his dirt-stained cheeks. "It was temporary insanity."

Elton wiped away the tears and sat up straight, locking on Briggs' eyes. "Okay, I've fessed up, opened my Kimono. You owe me that pain-free death you offered. I would never admit the truth publicly, and I'm at the end of life's cul-de-sac. I can see a sign flashing Dead-End."

"I'm not helping you die today, Frank. Too many unanswered questions."

"Like what?"

"Like, why you don't get a job teaching at Juilliard, where you trained? Why not stop drinking, go home and apologize to your wife and daughter, and rebuild your life?

Elton could offer no answers. "I'm tired," said Frank. "I need to sleep."

"Okay," said Briggs. "I'll come back tomorrow for the answers to my question. Then, after that, if you still want to die, I'll help you."

A half-hour later, Briggs walked into his Gold Coast townhouse.

"What's the verdict?" Jenny asked.

"Elton is a stubborn man who won't allow himself to grieve. He can't wait to meet the grim reaper."

7

B riggs filled in Jenny on the real story behind Elton's accident.

"Losing your fingers in a drunken accident is beyond sad," said Jenny. What are you going to do?"

"I've made an appointment with William Goldman, the conductor of the Chicago Symphony. He and Elton were best friends. I hope Goldman can offer ways to pull Elton out of his death spiral. Any news from Juilliard?"

Elton had been among the elite graduates at Juilliard, rated by many the nation's top school for the musical arts.

"I got a return call from the dean of the college, George Nyman, a friend and contemporary of Elton," said Jenny. "Nyman said Frank's accident was a huge loss to the music world. He pledged to help any way he could."

"Did he offer a teaching position?"

"He said Frank might not be able to play, but he can inspire a new generation of violinists. He'll have an honored place on the faculty. If they can find funding, they may even establish a chair in his name." Briggs smiled.

"Of course, I asked Nyman a dumb question or two

about what was so special about the violin and what it takes to master the instrument. He referred me to a website to learn more. Then he asked an odd question: did I watch golf? I admitted I didn't but said I knew the names of the big stars."

"How did he connect the violin to golf?" said Briggs.

"It's all about touch, Like Tiger Woods making an impossible putt from 70 feet away. Precise movements in Tiger's hands, fingers, and legs—calculated and controlled by his brain—send the golf ball 30 feet to the right, up a hill, then down a hill at the perfect speed, dropping into the middle of the hole. By comparison, Dean Nyman said that if you incorrectly place your finger one-hundredth of an inch, the violin will sound out of tune. He said it is one of the toughest instruments to learn and master."

"It's magic," said Briggs.

After hearing the options for Elton's future and the support he would likely get from other musicians, Jenny suggested contacting the man's estranged wife and explaining the situation.

"I'll do it, woman-to-woman. I'll paint a picture of a new, bright future, leaving out Elton's plan to exit this world if we can't convince him to go home and start over. I'm sure she wouldn't like a veterinarian ending her husband's life as if he were a stray dog. How many people would?"

"We have a plan," said Briggs, then moved in for a kiss.

"What will I do without you?" she asked.

Briggs had decided to leave his Chicago practice for his hometown, Portland, Oregon. He wanted Jenny to come with him. He proposed marriage and said they could establish a mobile canine care business.

"You can come with me," he said. "It would be easy to jump on a plane and visit your family anytime you like.

Oregon is a beautiful place with better weather. Better than Chicago's winters by a mile."

"The door is still open," she said. "Let's keep talking."

THE NEXT DAY, Briggs took the morning off from his clinical practice. He drove to Orchestra Hall at Symphony Center, the Chicago Symphony Orchestra home. He arrived just as a practice session for an upcoming concert had finished.

Goldman spotted Briggs and called him up to the stage.

Briggs walked over and looked around. At 6 feet 6, he was accustomed to dwarfing everything and everyone around him. He was a Lilliputian on a giant stage in an enormous hall with more than 2,500 seats. It took his breath away.

"Welcome, Dr. Briggs," Goldman said, offering his hand. Goldman's grip was firm, not what Briggs had expected from a man whose delicate touch with a baton controlled, directed, and inspired 93 performers, including 20 violinists.

"Where would Frank be standing?"

Goldman led Briggs across the stage. Briggs turned and took in the sweep of seats. "I'm in awe," said Briggs.

"Now pretend you're Frank, and every one of the seats is filled. Around you are 93 performers, including 19 other violinists, led by the concertmaster, which had been Frank's job. Next to the conductor, the concertmaster is the most important person for producing great music."

Briggs had accompanied Jenny to a few concerts, hardly the credentials for someone trying to understand Frank Elton's world. Or rather, his former world.

"Try to imagine the energy you feel when every seat is filled. And imagine the stress for our performers who play the equivalent of three concerts a week. Expectations are sky-high. Every performance is like the opening of a new play on Broadway. A great performance one night—even with the same cast of characters—doesn't mean the next night will earn raves."

"Did you say you're a veterinarian and wanted to discuss Frank's work and accident?"

"Yes, I'm a vet at Paws Care Emergency Clinic."

"How is Frank associated with a veterinarian?"

"Let's go someplace private," said Briggs.

He followed Goldman to his office.

After closing the door, Goldman admitted he knew about Frank's struggles and was trying to help him. He had urged Frank to take a vacation. Frank refused. Said he could play his way out of it. Goldman didn't know how his friend and concertmaster actually lost his fingers. Goldman was stunned when he learned the truth. He sat quietly for a moment before tears began streaming down his face.

"I love Frank. I'm heartbroken over his loss. We've been friends forever. At least he's alive."

"Barely," said Briggs. "He's alone and desperate to escape his mental anguish. He wants to die and is on the verge of suicide." Briggs didn't want to say more for fear of incriminating himself.

Goodman said he had been grieving the loss of his friend, sure the man was dead since all efforts to contact him the past two years had failed. He was shocked to hear what had become of him and agreed to help in any way he could. They hatched a plan.

8

V eterinary clinic work consumed Briggs' and Jenny's days. At night, they continued working to secure Elton's future. They agreed they would never publicly reveal the real story behind his accident. They felt certain Bill Goldman would tell no one. It was a week before Briggs returned to the homeless encampment. Jenny came with him after she agreed to take over his practice helping the dogs of the homeless, if not the role of the angel of mercy.

On their way to see Elton the next day to discuss his alternatives to death, Briggs stopped to visit Mayor Powell.

"Dr. Jim, great to see you. Who's this young lady trailing you?

"This is my colleague at Paws Care, Dr. Jenny Morrison." He left out the girlfriend title.

"I would invite you both in for tea, but there's not much room in my tiny apartment, and I have no tea."

They laughed.

"How's your little girl's tummy?" Briggs said.

"Sofi dog is back to her feisty self."

"Remember, no more Cheetos," he said, playfully wagging a finger.

"Of course not," Mattie said, raising her eyebrows.

Hey doc, have you seen Frank Elton?"

"We're on our way to lay out a plan for a future that doesn't include crossing the black divide.

"Great news. What happened to him is a tragedy. I talked to him about the accident. After a few shots of whiskey, he came clean with me. Figured I wouldn't tell anyone." Briggs nodded.

"But then a dark cloud crossed his face, and he warned me that he would kill me If I ever revealed the truth."

"Frank is coming unhinged," said Briggs. "I better get up to his place and talk to him."

"Good luck."

"Thanks. We'll need it."

Briggs arrived at Elton's tent five minutes later, ready to deliver the good news. If Frank pushed away all the offers for help, Briggs would give him what he wanted. He could come back after dark and deliver the fatal shot. Would he jump at the chance to teach at The Julliard, regaining some glory for all her dedication toward the perfection of his music?

If he took the job, Briggs and Jenny would buy him a new wardrobe, pay for flights to New York for him and his family, and loan them a no-interest down payment on a large apartment.

Jenny found an innovative prosthesis company that could fashion new, lifelike fingertips to replace his missing digits. Of course, they would lack the touch necessary to play the violin. Still, they could remove the distraction and embarrassment of the finger stubs.

Elton would also have time to reintegrate into society,

including the completion of a rehab program for his addictions and his diminished physical condition.

What wasn't to like? Frank Elton could choose life over death.

"Frank, are you there?"

"I'm here, and I'm sober."

Thank God for small favors, Briggs thought. Our job just got easier.

"Frank, put on your jacket and come outside. The sky is blue, and there is some actual warmth in the air."

A moment later, Elton emerged. His hair was cut, his beard gone. He was dressed in clean jeans and a long-sleeve red, checkered, flannel shirt.

Briggs and Jenny did a double take.

Without an explanation, Elton hugged Jenny, then Briggs.

"You want to know what changed?"

They nodded.

"Bill Goldman came by yesterday morning. I was embarrassed as hell for him to see me here, but he pushed away my objections. He drove me to his home to take a shower and shave, then gave me clean clothes. He paid for a haircut, and then we went to lunch. I guess you could say he talked some sense into me. He told me I could get a teaching position at The Julliard despite my injury and my stupidity for not listening to him and taking time off. He said he had worked out a plan with you and Jenny."

For the next hour, Briggs explained the plan. Jenny talked about her conversations with Elton's wife. Elton listened with few questions.

"Are you ready to be back in the world?"

"I am."

"Your wife and daughter are excited, too.

"Knowing Bill is still my best friend and supporting me after what I did flipped a switch in my head. I suddenly wanted to make him proud."

"Let's get out of here," said Briggs. Right now. Leave this for someone else." Elton nodded as he entered his tent and began filling a tattered backpack with the few personal items he had kept from his life as a master violinist.

"We have one more stop," said Briggs. "Let's say goodbye to Mattie Powell and her dog."

9

J enny Morrison had two reasons to celebrate—and a reason to grieve.

Saving Frank Elton and Rob Merritt—knowing the good things ahead for them—made her chest burst with pride. She was so happy Jim didn't have to kill another person that she burst into tears of joy. They hadn't solved the homeless problem or influenced that many lives. But the few people they helped made the risk worth it.

Launching former Concertmaster Frank Elton into life, with a new job and reunion with his family, filled her with warmth. He would soon have new prosthetic fingertips and an honored faculty position at The Julliard School.

Rob Merritt also got a reprieve, moving out of Lazy Acres to Southern California for cancer treatment. Several rounds of chemotherapy could arrest the cancer and prevent its spread, his oncologist predicted. A billionaire with unlimited resources and a world of possibilities his survival would benefit mankind. Jenny couldn't wait to see his future. And they had a feeling that Merritt would fund the Julliard chair for Frank Elton. After all, they had survived Lazy Acres and were headed for better times.

What grieved Jenny was the impending loss of Jim Briggs, the man she had meet six years before. Both started as interns at Paws Care Emergency Hospital and worked their way into full partnerships. Along the way, they fell in love and moved in together. She wished she could say 'the right rest is history,' as if they had lived happily ever after.

Sadly, it appeared there would be no future for them. No marriage. No children. The thought pressed down on Jenny's chest like a vise squeezing her heart.

Why was he leaving?

He hated the cold Chicago winters and was desperate to return to the Pacific Northwest and Portland, Oregon, where he grew up. He dreamed of starting a mobile canine care business, escaping the daily grind of veterinary hospital work.

She dreamed of big family dinners with the kids she and Briggs would have playing with a dozen cousins.

An upcoming canoe trip would be the getaway they needed to try to convince one another to go West or stay in Chicago.

BRIGGS AND JENNY packed up for a canoe trip on Lake Superior the next day. They would spend two weeks alone, enjoying the fresh air while deciding their future together.

They held hands as they looked forward through the windshield, about to head to the airport and to an uncertain future — and the possibility of losing one another.

Briggs looked over and smiled at Jenny. "Let's see where this trip leads." She offered a weak smile. Before he could put the car in gear, Briggs's phone rang. "Dr. Briggs, this is Jim Connell, your mother's pulmonologist. Ruby Joyce is on life support and doesn't have much time left. You must come now if you want to see her before she passes."

"If I can get a direct flight to Portland tonight, I can be there in the morning," said Briggs.

Briggs disconnected and started to explain.

"I heard him, Jimmy. You've got to go. You'll just have to return for our trip in the fall or next year."

That's not what he wanted to hear. He could see his chance of a life with Jenny slipping away.

10

J im Briggs and Jenny Morrison surveyed the supplies in their 17-foot canoe. Satisfied they had everything they needed for a two-week camping trip in Lake Superior's Isle Royale National Park, just this side of the Canadian border, they looked at each other and smiled.

Jenny pulled back her shoulder-length brown hair and tied it into a ponytail. Jim walked over, gently cupped her chin, and lifted her head to see her green eyes. He kissed her lips lightly.

"I love you," he said. She took a deep breath and said, "Me, too."

"To be continued," Jim said.

"Let's do it," said Jenny. He nodded.

She climbed into the front, adjusted water-tight supply bags at her feet, took hold of her paddle, and held it inches from the waterline, ready to launch. Jim grabbed the rear of the boat, gave it a hard shove, and jumped in. Normally, their Golden Retriever, Molly, would be with them. Instead, they left her with friends so they have more private time.

In the natural rhythm of competitive racers, they dipped

their paddle tips so expertly they barely made a ripple. The reward for their near silence was a symphony of natural sights and sounds.

Jenny spotted a Bull Moose drinking at the shore an hour after launch.

"How magnificent is that?" she whispered to Jim, trying not to spook the animal.

Jim mouthed a silent "Wow!"

The moose raised his head, standing tall, then snorted; he used his antlers and hooves to kick up sand toward the invaders. He was ready to fight. It was the first of myriad natural wonders they would witness before reaching their first-day destination five miles distant.

When Jim left Chicago three months earlier to start a new life and veterinary practice in Portland, Oregon, Jenny had stayed behind. He was gone before either realized the possibility of never meeting again. Then, Jim was back for the vacation they had postponed as if they had never been apart.

They had talked little during the day on the lake, except to point out animals or landmarks. The conversation was easy despite speaking very little on the phone during their separation. For the half hour they ate lunch—their boat drifting—they stared into each other's eyes with hardly a blink, as if trying to see into each other's soul, searching for the answer to where life would take them.

They steered into Birch Island Campground in the early afternoon and dragged their boat ashore. With only one tent site, they knew they would have the remote campground to themselves. After securing the canoe, they located the pad for their tent and spent the next hour setting up camp.

"I think we're done," said Jim. "The fire is set, and dinner is thawing. "You know what time it is, don't you?"

"It's wine-o-clock," said Jenny, smiling. "I'll get the wine, and you get the snacks."

"I'm on it," said Jim.

She filled two plastic glasses with white wine from a container while he retrieved a pre-packaged charcuterie of meats and cheeses for their sunset lounge, the name they gave their pre-dinner wind-down.

They sat beside each other, watching the sun slide into the lake, bumping glasses, saluting love and Mother Nature. Dinner included pasta with smoked salmon and a bagged Caesar salad. They saved Bailey's and hot chocolate for their dessert.

"Give me your hand," said Briggs. He helped her up, then led her away from the fire, through a thicket, to a log seat on the water's edge.

The mirror-like lake surface reflected the endless spray of stars above. Heaven and earth were one, a seamless portrait with no beginning and no end. They sat side by side drinking in the view while finishing their Bailey's. No words could describe the beauty. Their silence said it all.

Jenny leaned over and kissed Briggs on the lips, cupping his face with both hands. She didn't want to let go of the moment.

"Come with me," she said, taking his hand and leading him back to the fire. She pulled their sleeping bags from the tent, spread them out on the ground, and undressed, her naked body an invitation. Briggs accepted and climbed out of shorts and sandals.

"Imagine the rest of our life like this," said Jenny, her hands drifting to Jim's body.

"Right there," he said, directing her fingers. She grabbed his hand and pushed it between her legs a moment later.

"That's the sweet spot," she said, moaning softly."

"Jenny, should we ...?" He gasped and stopped talking. Their passion was its own heat. No campfire was necessary.

After they cooled down, they climbed into their sleeping bags.

They greeted the next day with a swim in the lake before dressing, then boiled water for coffee and prepped a breakfast of ham and eggs. Witnessing the rush of wildlife coming awake, with birds diving for food and fish rising for bugs, Jim smiled and said, "Life doesn't get better than this."

"Better together," he said. Jenny looked up at Jim, absorbing his words, and nodded.

"Maybe we can figure out a way to spend our life together after all," she said, then frowned and began sobbing.

"What's the matter, Jen?"

"I want us to be together more than anything," she said, a hitch in her voice, wiping her eyes on her sleeve. "Dad's got ALS. I can't leave him."

Briggs wrapped Jenny in his arms. She buried her head in his chest and cried.

He wanted to comfort her by promising he would move back to Chicago and share the burden of her dad's care. Something stopped him despite her anguish and his need to soothe her pain. Rather than offer empty promises, he said nothing. Instead, he listened to her recount the tense past six weeks since the diagnosis. The progression would be quick with severe disability assured within one to two years. Death was likely in three years, she explained.

As his mind juggled the possibilities, a made-made sound pierced the tension. Jenny's satellite phone, which she carried for emergencies, trilled. She let it ring until it stopped, in no hurry for the incoming message, which likely was bad news about her father. Briggs stood up, pulled her up by both arms, and hugged her.

"Let's wash your face," he said.

"Thank you. I'm okay. I can do it."

She pulled the bandana off her neck, wetted it, and washed and dried her face. Jenny waited for a minute more and checked her voicemail. She took a deep breath and returned the call.

"Jenny, it's Bill." Bill Morrison was the founding partner of Paws Care Emergency Hospital.

"A police detective was here today looking for you. It has something to do with the death of Mattie Powell. She wouldn't tell me how your name came up in her investigation."

She called him back and he picked up on the first ring.

"Are you saying Mattie is dead? It can't be. I saw her a few days ago, and she was fine."

"I'm as shocked as you are," he said.

"How did it happen?"

"Stabbed to death," said Bill, his voice a whisper.

"Did you say she was stabbed?"

"I'm afraid so. I have no other details. Detective Smith wouldn't say more."

"Oh Bill, I'm heartsick. She was a beautiful little lady. Why would anyone kill her?"

"Sorry for your loss," he said, offering no answer.

"Thanks, Bill. I'll tell the detective what I know, which isn't much."

She hung up and walked back to share the news with Jim.

"Mattie Powell is dead. The cops want to talk to me."

"Was that you?" he asked.

Jim wasn't surprised Mattie was dead. She had asked

him to terminate her life if she was gravely ill or if street life dragged her into a mental abyss. That was the promise of the Angel of Mercy. Once Jim moved, Jenny agreed to assume the angel role. So far, no one had qualified for the compassionate assisted suicide Jenny offered.

Jenny shook her head. "She was murdered, stabbed."

Briggs' mouth fell open, his face a twisted grimace. He was speechless.

"We need to go back to Chicago," said Jenny. "We've got to help police find the killer."

She stood up, undressed, and beaconed him toward the tent.

"Let's create one more memory—one more reason to stay together. I don't want my last memory of paradise to be Bill's call."

An hour later, exhausted, they climbed out of the tent and walked into the cool lake water.

"Close your eyes," Jenny said. "Fill your mind with last night's view of the stars in the lake." She closed her eyes, sank into the cool water, and began swimming away from the shore.

They reluctantly packed up and climbed into the canoe, heading home.

With long, slow strokes—stopping to watch wildlife, eat lunch, and swim—they returned to the launching ramp before dark.

11

C hicago PD Detective Shondra Smith tightened her weightlifting belt, pulled up her knee sleeves, and adjusted wrist supports. In front of her was a barbell weighing 320 pounds. For a 125-pound powerlifter, the weight was nowhere near a record; she was working up to that for an upcoming competition. But every attempt at a new weight silenced the gym, fellow officers stopping their workouts to observe Smith's attempt.

She walked over, snatched the weight to her waist, and lifted it cleanly over her head without a wobble before dropping it on the mat. A cheer erupted. Smith nodded and smiled. Just as she prepared for a second lift, her pager buzzed a 9-1-1 tone; Chief of Detectives Jean Blackman texted, "Get your ass back to the bureau, STAT.

"On my way," Smith typed.

Despite the boss's demand for an urgent response, Smith took her time, showering, patting her corn rows dry, then dressing. Although her dark chocolate skin was flawless and her lashes naturally long, she applied some makeup before finishing with a final touch of coral lipstick.

"Now I'm ready to eat shit," she said to her reflection. If nothing else, she would look nice for her ass whipping.

Detective Smith took the elevator the homicide division on the third floor and waded through a sea of cubicles—filled with surly, overworked investigators—to the chief detective's office.

"What's up, boss?"

"It's about time you got your ass in here," Blackman said. "Do you understand that when I text STAT, I mean now?" An old lecture Smith could recite in her sleep. She nodded and looked down like a dog caught peeing on the carpet. The feigned subservience was enough to settle down her boss, whose shoulders relaxed and voice dropped.

"Let me guess, you figured I was going to rip you a new one and decided to delay the pain," Chief Blackman said.

"Something like that," Smith admitted casually, with no sign of fear or urgency. Besides, she'd gotten used to Blackman's frequent blowups and grumpy demeanor the three years since Smith earned her detective shield. Five years patrolling the mean streets of Chicago—with its 700 to 800 murders a year—had thickened her hide. Once a meek, fearful rookie, she now thought of herself as Rhino Woman.

"I have a report on my desk with a note that suggests you're kicking a case back to me for reassignment." Blackman had a murderous look in her eyes.

Smith made her eyes look big. Was it a look of surprise or a taunt, like Muhammad Ali, who would drop his hands and dare his opponent to punch him? Blackman couldn't tell.

"Since when did you earn captain stripes?"

"Chief, I have a shitload of crime reports on my desk like every other detective. The last thing I need is the case of a homeless drug addict who died. They're a dime a dozen. It's dog shit, and I don't want it all over me."

"Close the door," Blackman said, her voice softer.

Blackman stood up, walked around her desk, and stood before her office window, surveying the roomful of detectives.

"Shondra," she said, shaking her head. "You've got a giant pair of balls. And, from what I hear of your weightlifting achievements, they're bigger than any big man around this place."

"Thanks, Chief. I'll take that as a compliment."

"Detective, I'm getting pressure from the brass to invest more of our few resources in disadvantaged communities. It's not a request. It's a mandate. You're the one I want on this case, along with your pretty face and your uncanny ability as a problem solver—and all-around snake charmer. You're the person I NEED on the case."

"Since you're sweet-talking me, I might find time in my busy schedule to peruse the file." Blackman smiled.

"We need to look like we care," she said. "Deep down, we all like to get justice for every victim. In a city like this, so big and unruly, there's no way to achieve that goal."

"Shondra, have you ever body surfed?"

"No, never seen the ocean."

"When a towering wave is bearing down on you, your first instinct is to panic and run. You may die if you run, the water's power and weight smothering you in the sand. So, you never run. Instead, you dive into the face of the wave or float right over the top. I know because I've experienced it and am lucky to be alive."

Smith cocked her head. The Chief had gotten her attention.

Blackman continued, "As police, we face unending waves. Our lives are forever inches from death. We need to avoid getting crushed. You understand?"

Smith nodded and said, "I'll get the murder book started, do a quick background check on the victim, review the evidence box, and talk to officers at the scene."

"You do that, detective. And remember that on Friday night, you'll join the Double Shooters at the firing range, followed by multiple rounds of beer and tequila."

"The high point in my week," she said, fist-bumping Blackman. Double Shooters was downtime for black detectives.

"Now, get on the case, STAT. I need results to report up the chain."

ASSEMBLING the facts for the murder investigation was easy. No eyewitnesses had come forward. That wasn't surprising, given the frayed relationship between the cops and the unsheltered.

The forensics team found an antique butcher knife with a pig carved into the handle, believed to be the murder weapon. Either the perpetrator panicked and rushed from the scene or left it to make a point; they may have wanted the world to know the attack was payback. But for what?

According to the coroner, the victim, Martha "Mattie" Powell, put up a fight, noting that the number of wounds suggests a crime of passion rather than a robbery gone wrong.

One digital photo showed a pile of paper from shredded books beside the body. Smith enlarged them on her computer screen and saw a name on a torn cover. Martha Marion Powell. The author?

Smith was puzzled, sure she had the wrong person's file. This Powell couldn't be the so-called "mayor" of Lazy Acres. Had the author turned homeless addict? No way.

She located Powell's author page in Amazon books with covers of her novels. A second search found dozens of articles, interviews, and photos. Comparing publicity photos and the victim's face, she knew they were the same.

"Holy shit," said Smith, remembering that she had read most of the books in Powell's detective series.

Smith had attended an author event and got a signed copy of Powell's most recent novel. She had her picture taken with the author. When Smith came forward to get her book signed, she told Powell she was a cop and wanted to write a series based her experiences. Powell had put her arm around Smith, placed a hand on her chest, and said, "All you need is what's right here. You can do it. Don't let anyone discourage you. Dream big."

Smith jumped up from her desk and stumbled over her trashcan as she race-walked into Chief Blackman's office.

"You won't believe this. My victim is Martha Marion Powell." Blackman cocked her head, waiting for more.

"Powell is a New York Times bestselling author. She disappeared five years ago after a very public divorce. Apparently, she's been homeless ever since."

"Holy shit, a celebrity. Just what we need."

"What do we do, Chief?

"Call the media department. Tell them what we have. But leave the media contact to them. Do not broadcast anything to those loudmouths," she said, pointing to the room of detectives under her command.

"Shonda, if we solve this one, we'll be heroes. The division will gain credibility. We'll get medals. Let's work the hell out of it. I'll run interference with the brass."

"I'm on it, Chief."

12

J im and Jenny's two-week canoe adventure in Isle Royale National Park had ended little more than 24 hours after launch. Their night together, naked, making love under the stars, left no doubt that they belonged together. Still unresolved was who would uproot and move so they could create a permanent life together. Would they choose Portland or Chicago?

The negotiation over a permanent home ended when Jenny revealed that her dad had been diagnosed with ALS and her mother's COPD was worsening.

"I can't leave them," she said. "The entire family is ready to help with their care, but no one is prepared to deal with the medical complications. That's my burden and gift to my parents, whose optimism powered my growth and career."

"There's no choice," said Jim. "You have to stay."

It was painful for him to tell her he was equally invested in his new life in Portland. His *Have Paws—Will Travel* mobile dog care van was nearly ready, and his marketing agency had secured 50 pre-paid customers waiting for his launch. Jim also had committed to community agencies and the Portland Humane Society to provide free care to the dogs of people experiencing homelessness.

Was his work life in Portland more important than a wife, children, and a life-long companion? Hell no, he wanted to say. A voice in his head told him to go west. Jim convinced himself that they would be together once her father passed if the love were strong enough. Deep down, he knew he was lying to himself. Three years apart would be an eternity.

"Jenny, I won't let you go," he pledged, though he knew they would drift apart like they had the past three months after he moved back to Oregon. The economics was only part of it, he said. "I feel an incredible emotional pull to Portland, the crazy politics, culture, and beauty."

"I wish I could say I understand. I have nothing to offer to change how you feel."

With doubt roiling their souls and clouding their future, they turned their focus to the murder of Mattie Powell.

Jenny pulled up a front-page Chicago Tribune article about Mattie's death.

Best-Selling Author Found Dead in Homeless Camp

CHICAGO, IL—New York Times Bestselling author Martha Marion "Mattie" Powell was found dead, an apparent victim of homicide, according to Chicago Police. She was 51.

Police say she was stabbed to death in her tent in the city's homeless enclave known as Lazy Acres, where neighbors say she reigned as unofficial mayor.

News of Powell's death and her homelessness left her friends and relatives in shock. Many knew she had disappeared but never knew where she went.

None of her homeless neighbors claimed to have seen or heard anything.

"When the unsheltered see us, their instinct is to run the other

way," a police source said. "One homeless man, who claimed to be a close friend of the victim, said she was nice to everyone. She could also be tough on troublemakers."

Evidence collected at the scene included a butcher knife believed to be the murder weapon.

A spokesman for Powell's publisher confirmed that after their author disappeared an automatic extension in her contract kept the books in circulation. Royalties are accumulating in an escrow account in Powell's name.

Police will hold a press conference later this week to update progress in the case.

If you have information you think might help the investigation, no matter how small, please send an email to WindyCity-Tips@chicagopd.org.

"I still can't believe she was stabbed to death," said Jenny, shaking her head. "Who would do that?"

"Her ex-husband or drug-addicted son?" Briggs suggested.

"You told me about how the husband's gambling drove him to leverage every last dollar of their wealth, including their two-million-dollar home," said Jenny. "I didn't know about the son. So, what's the story?"

Jim explained that when Mattie was living in her big home with money pouring in from book sales, she paid for her son's cocaine rehab several times and an apartment over her husband's objections. He claimed the money was for their future (secretly for his gambling debt). As a result, supporting their son was far down on the priority list—the perfect recipe for a failing marriage.

"After the bank repossessed her home and the bank and savings accounts were drained, Mattie was homeless. Her last family visitor was her son, who came begging for money and drugs," Jim recalled. "She had nothing to give. He didn't believe her, pushed her down, and grabbed her purse. He got away with $40 cash. He didn't return, as far as I know."

"Jenny, we owe it to Mattie to tell the police everything we know," he said. "I'll give them a call."

"Just remember," she warned, "if Mattie's neighbors start talking about possible suspects, you can bet the Angel of Mercy will be among them. We could end up in prison for the other so-called victims police might dig up."

"It's a chance we'll have to take," said Jim. "Mattie deserved better."

13

D etective Smith dug around in her closet for a disguise, pulling out a hat, hoodie, sneakers, and jeans. The jeans appeared tattered but were from a designer brand that charged big bucks for the trendy look; the less you get, the more you pay, or vice versa.

Standing before a full-length mirror, Smith confirmed she was ready to begin the Powell murder investigation. She figured the street look of mismatched clothes might get a foot in a door or two before the folks at Lazy Acres sniffed cop and scampered away. But, on the other hand, a dark suit and jacket, with her gun and gold shield flashing, was a no-go.

Despite efforts to keep Powell's identity quiet, the press swarmed on the news. Not only were T.V. reporters airing past interviews, but they showcased every dirty little detail of her failed marriage and her son's addiction. Further complicating Smith's job were reporter interviews of Lazy Acre residents. For a few bucks or 15 seconds of fame, Powell's neighbors were all too happy to share their opinions about their so-called 'good friend and neighbor, Mayor

Mattie.' Most offered bullshit theories of her death. With the investigation starting and evidence scant, reporters took whatever they could get—real or imagined.

Smith's phone rang. Caller I.D. showed Detective Derek Morton.

"Derek, what's up?"

"The tip line got a call from an unidentified male who said we needed to talk to Jim Briggs, a veterinarian. He called the guy an angel of mercy. He says Briggs is always hanging around Mattie Powell. Briggs is a partner at Paws Care Emergency Hospital. His side gig is giving free care to the dogs of homeless people. So, he knows everyone in Crazy Acres."

"Derek, be careful using the term crazy when discussing the homeless. If the mayor had heard you, your head would be on a spike; you'd be a tourist attraction at Navy Pier. You might as well have screamed the N-word in the lobby at City Hall."

"Geez, Shonda. Sorry," he said. "I didn't mean to offend."

"I understand," she said. "It's Cop talk. But things are changing. We need to change with the times. Or we'll be extinct like the dinosaurs.

He gave her Briggs' contact number and hung up.

Smith put off making the call. Briggs could be her first suspect. She needed to know more about the guy's interaction with the homeless. He sounded like an angel, caring for their dogs at no cost. But a killing angel?

She started her interviews with a man who lived next to Powell. He said she was always sunny and helpful, but they spoke little other than an occasional good morning. He said he heard nothing the night she died, Shonda thought, because he wanders around the city all night, gathering food and cast-off items for his tent home.

"I got in about two in the morning," the man said, identifying himself as Mark Bone. The name sounded fake. But she didn't challenge him.

Over two hours, Smith gathered little except repeated references to Briggs as an angel of mercy. She looked up the term.

Noun. Angel of mercy (plural angels of mercy), a type of mercy killer, a caregiver who is a serial killer, and who practices mercy killing on both the willing and unwilling, knowing and unknowing, dependent only on the killer's sense of a patient's level of suffering from their illness.

"Damn," she said to no one. "They're suggesting Briggs is some kind of serial killer who puts people out of their misery."

He must mean putting dogs out of their misery, she thought. That would make more sense.

Smith felt like a dog chasing its tale. Her investigation was going nowhere, continually circling back to Dr. Jim, as his homeless clients referred to Briggs.

She pulled out the phone number Derek had given her and dialed.

"Dr. Briggs," the man answered.

"Dr. Briggs, this is Chicago PD Detective Shondra Smith. I'm investigating the death of Mattie Powell. I understand you knew her and doctored her dog."

"I was just getting ready to call," Briggs said. "My girlfriend and I were up in Michigan canoeing when she got a call from her boss that somebody had killed Mattie. We couldn't believe it. We loved Mattie. She was a bright light on a dark night."

"Who is 'we'?" Smith asked.

"Jenny Morrison is a veterinarian surgeon, like me. She's my girlfriend."

Without explaining more, Smith asked, "Could you and Jenny come talk to us, and help us with our investigation?"

"Of course," said Briggs. "Tell us when and where, and we'll be there."

They set up an appointment for 10 a.m. the next day.

Smith noted that Briggs seemed eager to talk with her. Was that a way to get inside the investigation and move the suspicion off him? She would know more tomorrow.

14

"I've got an emergency patient coming for surgery," Jenny Morrison said. Her patient was a 180-pound Saint Bernard hit by a car. "Call and leave me a message after you talk to Detective Smith."

"Will do, Jen."

Jenny kissed Briggs, wished him good luck, and said, "Remember, if you're asked why people call you an angel of mercy, tell them that occasionally you have put down a dog. And that you do it in a humane manner that eases the dog's pain and the emotional upset of the owner."

"Got it," said Briggs. "Go. I'll call you later."

"One more thing," said Jenny. "Your remember Bellah, the Chihuahua puppy we patched up a few months back?

"Did she make?"

"She did, and she's thriving in a new home."

"A big win for our team," he said.

Savoring the bit of good news, Briggs caught a cab to the police station, arriving at security 10 minutes early. By the time he passed the screening and metal detector, he was right on time. An officer at the front desk called Detective

Shondra Smith, who authorized Briggs to go up to the detective bureau.

"Wow," said Shonda, at 5 feet 7, nearly a foot shorter than Briggs. You're a big guy."

"Not the first time I've heard that," said Briggs, who smiled. As always, he was wearing a Hawaiian shirt, shorts, sporting a full red beard with his hair pulled back in a ponytail.

"Follow me," Smith said, leading Briggs to a conference room.

"Coffee?"

"Sure. Black."

"I appreciate you coming in," she said. "According to a half dozen residents of Lazy Acres, you knew Mattie Powell well. Apparently, you knew everyone there."

"You would, too, if you'd been working with them for the past five years."

Smith started the interview with a grenade. It would either fall unexploded or blow her case wide open.

"Why do people call you the Angel of Mercy?"

"Do they?"

"Yes. And my dictionary says an angel of mercy is a compassionate serial killer."

Briggs laughed. "Yes, that's me: saving dogs all day and killing homeless people all night. No wonder I'm so tired."

Smith swallowed a smile.

"Did you kill Mattie Powell?"

"Why would I do that?"

"You tell me."

"Let me tell you about my relationship with the unsheltered. And, by the way, you should know that I'm a resident of Oregon, here for a two-week camping vacation with my girlfriend."

Smith cocked her head. "You're not living and working in Chicago?"

"Nope. I moved away three months ago. My full-time veterinarian practice is in Portland."

"I thought you were the dog doctor at Lazy Acres."

Briggs revelation put Smith on her back foot.

"I was in Chicago for six years. I came for a one-year internship at Paws Care and stayed. The Lazy Acres gig was community service. My girlfriend has taken over my responsibilities. She's a partner at Paws Care and a veterinary surgeon. She would've come with me today but had emergency surgery to save a dog hit by a car."

Smith made a note to interview Jenny Morrison.

"How did you end up in Oregon?"

"My dad was a police crime reporter for the Portland, Oregonian. He moved us from the San Francisco Bay Area when I was a kid. I attended vet school at Oregon State."

He could see Smith's eyes narrow, and her jaw tighten. She studied him like she was inspecting a dissected earthworm. Briggs knew at that moment his alibi was going to hold up.

"Why did you return?"

"For love," he said, smiling, the last time he made love to Jenny filling his mind.

"You're smiling, Detective Smith. You're probably having a flashback of your own."

Smith flushed at the comment, all but invisible beneath her ebony skin.

He explained that the return was a vacation he delayed when he had to rush home three months earlier to see his mother one last time before she died.

"I'm sorry about your mother," Smith said.

"I returned a few days ago hoping that a two-week

wilderness trip with Jenny would allow me to convince her
to move west. We want to marry and have kids. But unfortunately, she can't leave Chicago because of her sick father. As
much as I love the people, the food, the beauty of the city, I
can't take another freezing winter. Portland is a small city
with lots of cultural activities. A big dog-loving town. Also,
many wealthy people are willing to pay hefty monthly fees
for concierge care for their pups. And the weather is better
than most people think."

"Why do people call you an angel of mercy?" Smith
repeated.

"Because I'm a nice guy, and I help their dogs for free?
Also, I suspect it's because I patch up the homeless as
needed and give them vaccinations and wound care. I even
provide food. Occasionally, I put down one of their sick or
injured animals."

"Since when were veterinarians licensed to provide
medical treatment to humans?"

"We aren't," said Briggs. "I'm a licensed paramedic,
working under a local physician."

Smith thought Briggs' explanation made sense. But did
that eliminate him as a suspect?

Where were you three nights ago?"

"Last week, I flew from Oregon and spent a few days
preparing for our canoe camping trip at Isle Royale. We
launched two days ago and spent a night on Birch Island, a
secluded spot with no other campers. Jenny's partner called
her satellite phone and told her about Mattie's death and
your request to talk to her."

Again, nothing suspicious. A good alibi: canoeing
hundreds of miles away from the murder scene. Could he
have killed Martha Powell and then left for the trip?

"Do you know anyone who would want to harm Mattie

Powell?"

"Mayor Powell spent full-time looking out for other residents. Her tent was Grand Central Station for the community. She helped find resources for Lazy Acres residents and alerted me when a dog was sick or if someone needed medical help. Mattie had a rough relationship with her son, who showed up one day looking for money and drugs. He is or was a recovering addict. He hit her and stole $40 from her purse. Her husband, who wiped out their fortune to support a gambling habit, came by trying to get her to sign papers so he could control her book contracts and royalty accounts."

"How did that go over?"

"Mattie said she broke down, laughing hysterically. Then, he stormed out and said he would get her someday."

"He said that? He used the words 'get her'?"

"According to Mattie," Briggs said. "Detective, do you have suspects?"

"We'll check out the husband and son, of course. We'll continue to interview residents of Lazy Acres and hope someone comes forward."

"My dog care service in Portland, *Have Paws—Will Travel*, is launching in the next few weeks. Until then, I can wander around the camp, check on old friends, and see what they say about Mattie's death. I'll be staying with Jenny Morrison."

"If you learn anything new, you let me know immediately, no matter how insignificant it may seem. And don't be a hero and try to make an arrest."

"Of course, detective. I promise to stay out of your way."

They stood up and shook hands.

"I'll have Jenny call you," Briggs said.

"I would appreciate it," said Smith, walking him to the elevator.

"Aloha," she said.

He heard that a lot since he wore Hawaii shirts year-round. The red one he wore today drew more comments than the others.

"This shirt was my mother's last Christmas gift to me, just months before she died. I wore it on Mother's Day, the day they removed her from life support."

Smith cringed. "Sorry," she said.

"No need," said Briggs. "Imagine what the nurses thought the day I wore it into the CCU to unplug Mom. I looked like a guy who got lost on the way to a luau." He smiled and nodded as the elevator doors closed.

Briggs sighed in relief, convinced the angel of mercy angle was a dead end in Detective Smith's mind. At least he could hope.

Detective Smith called Jenny Morrison, got a recording that she was in surgery, and would return the call as soon as possible. "Leave me a message."

"This is Detective Shondra Smith of the Chicago Police Department. Dr. Briggs said you might have information to help me with the Mattie Powell murder investigation. Please call me so we can set up a time to meet." She left her mobile number.

Two minutes later, Morrison returned the call. "Sorry, detective, just coming out of surgery. We tried like hell to save this Saint Bernard. She was too badly injured. As an emergency hospital, most of our cases are life or death. Luckily, more live than die."

"I'm sure it's no fun to tell an owner their animal died," said Smith.

"That's the hardest part of the job."

Morrison agreed to an interview.

"See you tomorrow, Detective Smith."

15

D etective Shondra Smith sat at her desk reviewing the information she had gathered for the murder book.

Creating a murder book was essential training for new detectives; Smith, a detail freak who found comfort in a system designed to reduce the chaos of juggling multiple cases at once, learned her lesson well. The murder book was her friend, like a therapy dog. She rubbed her hand over the smooth front cover and closed her eyes as if it were a genie who could grant her wish to identify Mattie Powell's killer.

The Los Angeles Police Department created the investigative tool in the 1980s to organize and standardize homicide case files. Investigative reports, photos, and other materials are added to the book in a uniform structure to make it easy for detectives, supervisors, and prosecutors to review and locate case information quickly and help manage the caseload.

Smith knew the file—given Powell's celebrity—would be a fire-breathing dragon for her to tame. So far, she had made little progress.

Smith opened the Murder Book and re-read the reports and notes.

An anonymous phone caller said Briggs was an angel of mercy. Briggs said it may have been a reference to the free medical care he provided to the homeless and their dogs. If that were true, why would someone offer it as a tip? Smith needed convincing.

An interview with Mattie Powell's neighbor claimed her heroin-addicted son, Eddie, attacked her and stole cash. Not surprisingly, Powell filed no police report. Besides, who would care about a homeless woman getting attacked and losing $40? No one.

The four most likely suspects were Jim Briggs, Jenny Morrison, Mattie's husband, Bernard Millwood Sr., and their son, Edward "Eddie" Millwood Jr.

Smith initially eliminated Briggs, who had been living in Portland and returned for a wilderness vacation with his girlfriend. However, she knew Briggs could have slipped into Powell's tent late one night and killed her. But, if he had a problem with the woman, wouldn't he have killed her as he exited Chicago three months before?

Smith couldn't get the angel of mercy comment out of her head. It was a serial killer, an individual helping people escape their misery. Briggs said he euthanized dogs as needed and maintained a supply of heart-stopping barbiturates. Given the high misery index at Lazy Acres, death could have been a welcome visitor among Chicago's lost and forgotten citizens.

Could Briggs have been killing on demand? If so, how could that have escaped Chicago PD? She knew precisely how. The homeless, although a constant source of police activity, were ghosts no one wanted to see.

Smith spun her chair toward her computer, logged in, and began a search for statistics on homeless deaths. She wasn't surprised to find dozens of websites dedicated to homelessness. The figures made her head spin. One estimate put Chicago homelessness at 65,000, with an annual death count of more than 1,200.

Briggs couldn't possibly kill a thousand people a year, could he? But a smaller number, like 50? Smith thought it was possible, given the system for investigating deaths in Chicago. She knew that an autopsy was at the discretion of Cook County Coroner Nancy Barruci. And Barruci wouldn't order one if the death was known to be of natural causes or if the individual's medical history indicated the likelihood of imminent death, and there were no signs of foul play.

If the coroner found a needle mark and barbiturate in the blood of a homeless person in poor health with drug addiction, no autopsy would likely be conducted. Why order an autopsy when, according to various data sources, drug overdoses have been a leading cause of death among homeless people?

The next day, Smith reviewed the murder book notes from Jim Briggs' interview as she prepared for her interview with Jenny Morrison. She would again press the angel of mercy angle. Mattie was stabbed to death, not euthanized. Still, there could be a connection. The stabbing could have disguised the actual cause of death.

Smith's phone played the music from Tina Turner's *What's Love Got to Do* with It hit.

"Detective Smith, this is Jenny Morrison. I'm downstairs in the lobby."

"I'll be right down to get you."

After settling in a conference room with coffee and

chitchat, Smith fired her first question, hoping it might break open her case.

"Why do people call Dr. Briggs an angel of mercy?"

"He told me you asked him that," Morrison admitted.

Smith should have expected Briggs and Morrison would talk. If the angel of mercy were a hot button for them, they would agree on an answer.

"Dr. Briggs says it's because he helps the homeless and their dogs for free."

"Until three months ago, I wasn't part of his homeless practice. I took over after he left. Jim was an angel, given the help he gave all those poor people."

"Dr. Morrison, you may be interested in the definition of an angel of mercy supplied by Wikipedia. Let me read it to you."

An angel of mercy or angel of death is a type of criminal offender (often a serial killer) who is usually employed as a caregiver and intentionally harms or kills people under their care. The angel of mercy is often in a position of power and may decide the victim would be better off if they no longer suffered from whatever severe illness is plaguing them. This person then uses their knowledge to kill the victim. In some cases, as time goes on, this behavior escalates to encompass the healthy and the easily treated.

"Jim's mother was a tireless homeless advocate in Portland and took Jim to a shelter weekly to help with meals and housecleaning, bedmaking, and other chores," said Morrison. "Helping the unsheltered was part of his education growing up, and a passion as an adult." She didn't tell the detective that Jack Kevorkian was one of Briggs' heroes.

"Still, I'm having a hard time figuring out why an anonymous caller would say we could look into Briggs as an angel of mercy."

"Was your anonymous caller someone who didn't get the help they thought they should get? People experiencing homelessness suffer myriad health problems, injuries from fights and accidents, and so many more hazards of street life. Why they focused on Dr. Briggs is anyone's guess."

"Where were you last Tuesday night?"

"Am I a suspect?"

"Anytime we investigate a murder, we ask anyone and **everyone** standard questions to build a picture of the victim's life. Think of it as a jigsaw puzzle that needs filling in. One of those pieces is the likely killer."

"I was at O'Hare, picking up Jim for our canoe trip," said Morrison. "We drove back to my place, had takeout, and went to bed, where we spent the evening catching up, if you know what I mean."

Smith's dark skin hid her red face. She was no prude. But the honesty surprised her.

"That's all I have at the moment. I may need to talk to you again. In the meantime, if you hear talk about Mattie Powell's murder while making your rounds at Lazy Acres, please call me."

Morrison nodded.

"By the way, Detective, veterinarians practice the same 'do-no-harm' philosophy as medical doctors do with humans. Next to losing a dog in surgery, euthanizing a sick or injured canine is hell. We often do it with distressed family members watching, adding further stress. I can only imagine how hard it must be for doctors to assist with suicides."

Smith nodded as if she understood. After taking Morrison to the lobby, she returned to her desk, noting, "Angel of mercy could be someone who assists with suicides."

What the hell was Smith thinking? The Mattie Powell case and a dozen other murders were piling up on her desk. Why add another? She needed to solve the Powell murder before the mayor and police chief hammered her boss for lack of progress.

16

Because of his size—5 feet 1 and 110 Pounds—William "Little Billy" Wilson was belittled and battered his entire life. Other boys and men eroded his self-worth with insults like shrimp, short stuff, and the little guy. As in, "Hey, little guy, what's up?"

A grown man, he was forced to buy pants in the boy's department or find unisex shirts marked 'petite.' There was no escape once the nickname 'little' was attached to his name. He asked his friends to call him William, never Willie. They ignored him. He would always be their Little Billy. He had learned to live with it.

His mother added to his shame, telling her friends he was 'fragile as a sparrow.' She told his one serious girlfriend, Nancy, to 'be gentle with him.'

Nancy was two inches shorter than Billy and had also suffered humiliating comments over her height. But, standing next to one another, they appeared the perfect pair. Ultimately, she couldn't take the taunts from so-called friends about her 'little guy who undoubtedly has a tiny cock.'

"Billy is 12 inches," she exclaimed one time. Her best girl-friend Heidi's mouth dropped open before laughing; she was sure it was a joke. Heidi's boyfriend jumped into the conversation.

"You mean 12 centimeters, like this," he said, thrusting his middle finger in Nancy's face.

"Don't be cruel," said Heidi when she saw tears filling Nancy's eyes.

Eventually, Nancy couldn't deal with the taunts and took up with a bigger guy, married him, and had a baby—the outcome Little Billy had dreamed of when he and Nancy met two years earlier.

After Nancy, his life was a series of hookups on dating apps—primarily women who claimed to be horny and in sexless marriages. Billy liked that. Quick with no emotional attachment. Most were one-off dates. Some contacted him for repeats, telling him they loved that 'he was hung like a horse.'

One of his dates offered a backhanded compliment, noting, 'Who knew I'd be chasing a tiny guy with a big dick.' His manhood was a source of pride, especially on the few occasions when he'd be showering at the gym and another man would comment, loud enough for everyone to hear, "Hey, big guy, how's it hanging." It may have been recognition of his penis size or a cruel joke. Still, he liked the recognition that he was literally the biggest man in the room.

As a young man, Billy's Roman nose, cleft chin, and thick sandy hair turned heads. He looked like a miniature fashion model. Unfortunately, his size and shyness kept most girls at bay. A loner living in a single-parent home with a helicopter mother, his only escape was working as a shoe salesman in a department store. He made good money, which would have allowed him to get his own place. But what was the point? He didn't need privacy. And his mother did the cooking, cleaning, and washing—when she stayed sober for an hour or two. Occasionally, Billy washed the dishes. And he contributed $ 1,000 a month toward household expenses.

Management named him the best salesman five years in a row. His looks, size, and ability to gauge a woman's needs and fashion sense made him popular among customers and staff—until a customer accused him of looking up her skirt.

Her dress was so short her thong underwear left little to the imagination when she sat down to try on high heels. Placing shoes on her feet, Billy looked up to gauge her reaction to the style and fit, trying not to look at her exposed crotch. Out of respect, Little Billy made it his code of conduct to keep his eyes on the shoes and customer faces, especially with women flashing their privates. That wasn't enough for the customer.

After getting into a fight over the shoe price at the sales counter, the woman said the entire staff would be in trouble, especially the "little guy over there who looked up my dress." After the woman left the store, the cashier told Billy she was sorry, calling the obnoxious customer a prick tease.

After the woman complained, Wilson's boss fired him. No trial. No second chance. Two weeks' severance.

Despite his innocence, his mother accepted the customer's version of the story and chewed him out for immoral behavior. Police interviewed him and found no reason to investigate further. In their follow-up, the woman told police she felt the "little pervert" got what he had coming to him and had no interest in pursuing the matter.

Between the police interview and his mother's verbal beat-down, Little Billy hit rock bottom. He wanted to curl up and die.

"I hate you," he yelled, flipping off his mother as he stormed out the door of her home with a suitcase.

With no job and no home, he bought a backpack, tent, camp stove, and utensils, then took a bus to Lazy Acres. With his shiny store-bought equipment, he found an open space and moved in—a loser on his way to the bottom of life's darkest canyon.

Billy hoped the move would bring him peace. Instead, the other unsheltered residents shunned him, branding him an interloper. As he sunk deeper into depression, he got dirtier, let his hair and beard grow, and avoided brushing his teeth or lifting a finger to groom himself. Only then, at his lowest point, did neighbors view him as one of them.

They offered food, drink, and conversation. And everyone called him William, a sign of respect the housed world never gave him.

Before neighbors began to help, Little Billy lived on beer, pork rinds, and chocolate bars. Rob Merritt, his neighbor two tents down the row, was the one bright spot in his life. He was a frequent drinking buddy, regularly drowning their sorrows in alcohol.

Deep in their cups one night, Merritt said an angel of mercy would soon help him die. When Billy pressed for a name, Merritt revealed the angel was Dr. Jim, the veterinarian.

Desperate, Little Billy wanted what Dr. Jim was offering: a humane death.

"Gimme his number," Billy demanded, the six-pack of beer slurring his words.

"First," said Merritt, "you need the support of Mayor Powell."

"Who the hell is Mayor Powell?"

"She's that little woman a half mile down the row. Mattie

Powell has is the unofficial mayor of our lovely community, which she named Lazy Acres. Dr. Jim listens to her because she is good at prioritizing community needs. She's everywhere and tries to help everyone."

After recovering from a massive hangover the next day, Little Billy introduced himself to Powell and said he wanted to die. But when he told her his story—admitting he was healthy except for depression from a lifetime of shaming—she offered to get him therapy.

"Who the hell are you to decide who lives and dies?" Billy raged. The argument was loud, carrying far beyond Powell's thin tent walls.

"You can talk to Dr. Jim, but I know he won't do it. He turns down more requests than he accepts."

Billy finally arranged a meeting with Jim Briggs following his argument with Mayor Powell. "Mattie Powell was right. Death is a permanent solution to a temporary problem," said Briggs. "I'll help however I can, but I can't offer that."

After Briggs left, Billy slammed down a half dozen beers and muttered to himself, "Mattie Powell is going to pay for what she did."

A month later, Rob Merritt had moved out, Jim Briggs was opening a mobile canine service in Portland, Oregon, and Mattie Powell was dead.

17

A Chicago Tribune front-page story detailed plans for Mattie Powell's funeral and her rise to fame.

Because the murder involved a celebrity who had fallen from grace, the attendees were a mixed bag of who's who in Chicago and the not-so-important. The politically influential socialites and social justice advocates turned out in droves.

Advocates for the unsheltered used the occasion to generate donations and bolster their cause. A local pastor who operated a food kitchen for the homeless said, "This shows that no one is immune to this plague." Donations to his food kitchen jumped 50% following the publicity around the homeless writer's death.

Powell couldn't have imagined that her death would become a cause celeb for homelessness. Then again, she would have been pleased to know her work with people in Lazy Acres had paid off.

Detective Shondra Smith stood at the back of St. Mark's Cathedral, watching the well-wishers enter the church. She knew one could be the killer, there to silently gloat, pray for forgiveness, or gleefully witness what their dirty deed had wrought.

Among the mourners were Powell's publisher, old friends from her glory days as a best-selling author, and even one or two neighbors from Lazy Acres. Jim Briggs and Jenny Morrison acknowledged Detective Smith as they joined the procession.

Smith hadn't ruled out Morrison and Briggs as suspects. Their alibis seemed solid. The two had focused on each other and a long-delayed wilderness trip.

Briggs had left the area three months before, so he had no reason other than his girlfriend to return—at least none Smith could identify. Recognizing that the stabbing was a crime of passion, Smith's investigation shifted to Powell's husband, Bernard Millwood. Millwood was a failed author and popular creative writing professor at Northwestern University's Medill School of Journalism.

According to Powell's publisher, Millwood was pushing hard to get control of his wife's royalty account, which held more than a million dollars. He had threatened legal action if they didn't turn over the money. As Powell's spouse, he insisted he was her legal heir. Before the murder, the publisher's legal staff told him there was no indication that Powell was dead, so their hands were tied. Powell made her son heir to any money from book sales in her publishing contract, which the publisher didn't share with Millwood. Powell hoped the books would be a source of income for her son, a constantly recovering addict who rarely could—or would—work.

Medill's dean shared a rumor that Millwood was in financial trouble again over gambling debts, reinforcing Detective Smith's suspicion of the husband.

As funeral attendees took their seats, Smith spotted a

very short, shabbily dressed man pressing against a back wall as if trying to melt into the woodwork. Odd, she thought, surreptitiously photographing him with her phone camera. She opened the photo app and enlarged it. It was clear and sharp. Smith figured he was one of Mattie's neighbors from Lazy Acres. She would show the photo to Briggs.

When the services ended and the mourners moved to the gravesite, Smith edged her way to the back of the mass of people surrounding Powell's casket. If Powell had been any other unsheltered person whose body was unclaimed, it would have been cremated or donated to the Anatomical Gift Association. But, instead, Powell was escaping her world first-class, her publisher paying the tab.

The little guy Smith had spotted in the church reappeared at the burial site; this time, a tree partially hid him. Given the well-dressed city royalty attending the ceremony, she wasn't surprised he would want to melt into the landscape.

After the graveside invocation, Smith pulled Briggs and Morrison aside. She turned around and pointed out the man lurking in the background. He was gone.

"I want you to look at a photo and tell me if you recognize this man," said Smith, who enlarged the image on her screen.

"That's Little Billy," said Briggs, using the man's nickname."

"What's his last name?"

"It's Wilson. He's William "Little Billy" Wilson."

"How do you know him?"

"He was a patient."

"I thought you doctored dogs?"

"I do, of course. As I explained in our interview, I'm a licensed paramedic. I provide basic healthcare to those poor folks. Many, if not most, of the people experiencing homelessness are covered under various government-funded health programs but don't trust the system or can't navigate the paperwork needed to qualify for benefits. So, it's a mixed bag of reasons, from mobility issues to lack of transportation."

"What is wrong with Little Billy?"

Briggs explained Little Billy's firing and his downward spiral to Lazy Acres.

Smith made a note to check for police reports on the skirt incident.

"His problem was depression. He needed therapy and medication. Mattie Powell, who served as a referral point for those who sought my help, tried to discourage him from talking to me. I'm a paramedic, not a psychiatrist. Mattie told him she would connect him with mental health services. He insisted on a meeting with me. For drugs, I suspect."

"How did the meeting go?"

"He was angry when I told him for the fourth time that I wasn't a mental healthcare professional, and I wasn't about to give him drugs of any kind. Nor did I have access to psycho-therapy medications."

"Was he angry enough to kill Mattie Powell?"

"I can't speculate, detective, at what point a person might snap. I can tell you that Little Billy was severely depressed and, I suspect, looking for a way out."

Detective Smith stood up straight, on edge. "What do you mean, 'a way out.'?"

"He confessed that he felt betrayed by everyone, including his mother. He said he wanted to die."

"And you didn't offer to help?" Smith squinted and pinned Briggs with her eyes like he was a speared fish.

"As you pointed out, I doctor dogs and occasionally put them down humanely. However, I don't kill people."

Smith wasn't convinced but said, "Of course, I understand."

Briggs and Morrison said goodbye, leaving Smith with a new imperative: track down and talk to Little Billy Wilson, her latest suspect.

She couldn't let go of the idea that there may be something to Briggs as an angel of mercy.

18

W hen Bernard Millwood saw an incoming call from the Chicago PD, he dropped his phone and moved away from it like it was a poisonous snake.

He let it go to voicemail. Chances are, he thought, the cops wanted him to identify Mattie Powell's personal effects. Or his gambling debts had returned to haunt him, setting off alarms in the police department's vice squad. Had his bookie been arrested, naming Millwood as a regular customer?

Detective Smith left a number but didn't give a reason for her call. The lack of explanation panicked Millwood.

He took a deep breath and dialed Smith's number.

"Detective Smith, homicide bureau." The word homicide set off a wave of nausea.

"This is Bernard Millwood," he said, his voice quivering. "I'm returning your call."

"I'm investigating your wife's murder," Smith said. "I have some questions for you."

"Well, I certainly didn't kill my wife, detective, so you'd

be wasting your time talking to me." She couldn't see his shaking hands or the sweat running down his scalp, drops of hair dye streaking his face.

"It's routine to speak with a victim's family and friends as part of the investigation."

"What questions do you have?"

"Let's talk in person," said Smith.

"Is that necessary, detective? I know you've got more important cases to work on. Excuse me if I sound cold, but my wife chose to live as a homeless junkie. Like mother, like son."

Ignoring Millwood's rant, Smith said, "Our inquiries are routine. First, we must gather all the relevant facts and determine the best action plan. As you can imagine, my bosses want to end this case as quickly as possible."

Millwood softened when he sensed Smith's determination to close her case and move on."

"Well, I have a lecture at one this afternoon. You could come by my office at 2:30.

"I'll see you then," she said and hung up.

JUST AS SMITH reached for the door of Millwood's office, it opened, and a thin blonde woman in her early 20s walked out, tucking in her blouse. Her face was flushed. She used her sleeve to wipe something off the corner of her lip and looked away when she saw Smith.

"Thank you for your help, Professor Millwood," she said, scurrying down a long hallway.

"You're welcome, Mary. Keep up the good work."

"Come in, Detective Smith. Please sit down."

Smith looked around for a place to sit. Books filled all three chairs.

Millwood walked around his desk and cleared a spot for Smith to sit, then looked down and saw his zipper was down. He turned around, zipped up, then settled in his chair.

"How can I help you?" Millwood rushed the words as if he were a student about to be dressed down for failing an exam. "Any leads in my wife's case?" Millwood asked.

"We're still gathering evidence, as I said on the phone. So, I can't share specifics. It could jeopardize our case."

"I'm surprised you're pursuing a homeless homicide at all." Smith raised her eyebrows.

"Professor Millwood, where were you the night your wife died?"

"Martha and I are still legally married, but she left me years ago. I've moved on. I have a girlfriend and a new life."

"Was that your girlfriend?"

Millwood sighed. "If you must know, yes. She's my fiancé. And she's a graduate student supervised by another professor. So, I'm not breaking any rules."

"A former student?"

"Got me," said Millwood.

"Your wife just died, and you're already engaged?"

"Legally, I'm married. However, I haven't had any contact with Martha or lived as a married couple for years."

"You didn't answer my question."

"Detective, I can see you're good at your job with wonderful powers of observation. However, my social life isn't what you're here to discuss. So, let's move on."

"Everything is relevant in a murder investigation. Where were you?"

"With Mary Corrigan, my girlfriend, the woman you saw

leaving my office. We spent the night together. If you must know, we were in bed all night. She'll vouch for me."

"Good," said Smith. "I'll need to talk to her."

Millwood's shoulders slumped.

"Is that necessary? I want to keep her out of this mess."

"I'd appreciate her contact information," said Smith, ignoring his objection. Millwood stopped resisting and called out the number from memory.

"Professor, I understand you had a little problem recently with Ms. Powell's publisher. Tell me about that."

"The little problem is that they are illegally withholding family money from Mattie's book sales. Now that she is gone, I should have access to those funds and control any contracts related to future sales. It's a marital property we jointly owned."

"As I understand it, you've had a problem with gambling in the past," she said. "We know that you wiped out your savings and took out loans on your home to repay debts. As a result, your wife was left homeless and broke."

The truth was a punch in the chest. He was an addict then and still was. Now, faced with his wife's death and the fact he put her in jeopardy by leaving her homeless, Millwood wanted to hide under his desk. He closed and covered his eyes.

"I can't deny that it was a shitty thing to do. And I'm sorry for the consequences, but I've turned the corner. Mary is helping me stay away from my old vices. The money from Mattie's books will help us—I mean me—move forward." He could see the detective wasn't buying his lie.

Millwood suddenly felt like a trapped rat. He was angry and confused. But, dammit, he deserved the book royalties, didn't he?

"Any more questions, detective? I need to prepare for my next class."

"I have what I need for now. I may have more questions after I interview Ms. Corrigan. I assume you plan to be around."

"Of course, I'll be around," said Millwood. "I'm innocent. You don't have to worry about me fleeing the country."

"Good to know," said Smith, who thanked him and left.

Millwood phoned his girlfriend and told her to confirm his story that they were in bed all night. The truth, he knew, would put him in Smith's gunsights.

19

"Y ou don't look well," said Jenny, feeling Briggs's forehead.

"My stomach is burning, and my chest is tight," said Briggs, frowning.

"Talk to me," she whispered, nibbling on his ear.

"Life takes funny turns, doesn't it," he said.

"What do you mean?"

"Three months ago, we were sitting in my car, about to leave on our canoe trip, before I moved west. Our future together was on the verge. Lazy Acres was in the rearview mirror. And my dream of starting a mobile canine care business was forming."

"And now?"

"Now, a savvy Chicago detective has her eye on me as a suspect in Mattie's murder while zeroing in on the so-called angel of mercy. I'm inches from falling off a 1000-foot-high cliff. My future, which could have included marriage and a family with you, may include a life prison sentence."

Jenny sat on Briggs's lap, wrapped her arms around his neck, and squeezed.

"Don't be silly. And quit feeling sorry for yourself. I'm neck-deep in this bog with you. I'm nervous, too, about Detective Smith's sudden interest in the angel. But is there any physical evidence that you assisted the suicide of Lazy Acres residents? No."

"We both know that Illinois forbids assisted suicide, which technically wasn't what I've been doing the past few years," said Briggs. "The Cook County D.A. would charge murder. I guess I'm lucky there's no death penalty."

"See, there is a bright spot in this gray day," said Jenny, smiling, then kissing Briggs's lips. "Do you regret helping those poor people?"

"You know I don't. Still, I'd rather be canoeing with you and carrying you off to Oregon for a happy life."

"Don't get ahead of yourself. I have an idea how we can move the Powell murder investigation along and Detective Smith away from the angel of mercy angle."

"Please tell me."

"We'll contact Rob Merritt and ask for help," said Jenny. "We know he's recovered from his chemo and is back at work. He's a billionaire with nearly unlimited resources. He knows other people who were in the same situation as he was. He owes you—he owes us—his life. And I believe he would consider it a small favor."

"Maybe you're right."

"Wait until he hears about Mattie's death. He liked her. She guided him to you. He'll be all over this."

Looking at his watch, Briggs said, I'll call him now."

ROB MERRITT ANSWERED the moment he saw Briggs' number.

"My good Dr. Briggs, how the hell are you?"

"Rob, you sound great, like you're on a high."

"Talking me out of dying was an incredible gift. You gave me a new lease on life, and I'm enjoying every second. My cancer is in remission. My ex-wife and her husband are now my best friends. And business is booming."

"You're an amazing guy. You made the right choice."

"Thanks again," said Merritt. "Consider me your genie. Ask anything, and it's yours if I can get it or buy it."

"Thanks, Rob."

"Rob, did you hear about Mattie Powell?"

"I was out of the country until yesterday and just caught the news. I'm still in shock. Who would want to kill Mattie?"

"That's the question Chicago Homicide Detective Shondra Smith is asking. Unfortunately, during questioning the residents of Lazy Acres, my name has come up with several people calling me the angel of mercy. Not only am I a suspect in the murder because of my interaction with Mattie, but now this angel of mercy thing is hanging out there. The problem is I can't tell the detective about the people I assisted or those who wanted to die that I turned down. Or, one of those I turned down may have been pissed at Mattie and me."

"Oh, shit. That's not good. You were an angel for those of us you helped. You shouldn't be penalized for what you did. Who's the individual we're talking about?"

"One man in particular was angry at Mattie and me when I told him I couldn't help. He was depressed but otherwise healthy. Mattie and I both offered to find counseling. He wanted none of it. I left for Portland a week after our final encounter. The fact that I've been gone and living in Oregon for the past three months should be a rock solid alibi. I'm just not sure that Detective Smith believes that I that my return to Chicago to vacation with Jenny is a coincidence with Mattie's death."

"The guy you're talking about at Lazy Acres is Little Billy, right?" said Merritt.

"Yes, that's the man. Unfortunately, I can't point the detective toward him without implicating myself."

"I got loaded with him more than once and listened to hours of his drunken rants."

"Jim, don't worry. I've got a first-rate private investigator who will track him in no time. I'd bet he's at his mother's house. I'll find him and talk to him in person, if necessary. In the meantime, an anonymous tip pointing to Billy as a suspect in Mattie's murder might take the pressure off you and put him in jail."

"I feel better already. Thanks for your help."

"It's the least I can do."

"By the way, how's life in Portland?"

"It's my hometown. I love it. The only thing missing is Jenny. We want to get married and have children. Sadly, her father has a fatal disease, and her sisters are no help. We've promised to stay in touch when I return to Portland. I even proposed coming for monthly visits. But you can't commute 2,000 miles once a month and have a happy marriage. Or raise a family. Chicago is a great city, but the winters and non-stop canine emergency surgeries have burned me out."

"You're definitely in a bind. How about moving Jenny's Dad to Oregon, where she could still care for him?"

"The problem is getting specialists in place, then transferring him safely."

"There's no problem without a solution. I can help with that, too. But, first, let's get this detective off your back and solve the murder."

Rob filled in Jim on his conversations with William

"Little Billy" Wilson. When he finished, he said, "I've got your back."

20

Shondra Smith and her wife, Ingrid Bjerke, sat up in bed talking, drinking coffee, and reading the morning news on their tablets. They loved the wake-up routine. Their conversations were benign, a relaxing time before the morning work crush.

They played the mini crossword puzzle and spelling bee in the New York Times. They read comics and scanned the sports page. Shondra loved Chicago Bull stars Jordan, Rodman, and Pippen but felt a fondness bordering on lust for Steph Curry of the Golden State Warriors. But, of course, she would never say that to anyone but Ingrid, a soccer fan with little interest in hoops.

Mostly, their political views aligned with an occasional kerfuffle over a minor difference on climate change, LGBTQ+ issues, or world hunger.

They were a study in contrasts, physically and mentally: Ingrid, tall and thin, was an evolutionary biologist who taught classes at Northwestern University. Her master's level course covered 40,000 years of population migration; Shondra was short, less brainy, but an intelligent cop with a

B.S. in criminal forensics; Ingrid liked to read, while Shondra loved British TV police procedurals. Ingrid was a Swedish blond with pale skin and eyes, while Smith was a rich dark chocolate with Haitian roots.

Shonda and Ingrid relished their differences and enjoyed the smiles they drew in public. People often pulled them aside to ask how they got together like they were a curiosity in a fun house.

They met at a criminal justice course where Ingrid explained the value of DNA as an investigative tool. She showed a map of how DNA is used to identify where groups of humans originated, noting the role of climate in skin color and other human characteristics.

Piercing their morning serenity veil, Shondra's phone jolted her with a *Charge of the Light Brigade* ringtone. She needed to change that.

"Shit," it's Derek," she told Ingrid. "The news can't be good."

"What's up, Derek? It had better be important."

"Did I interrupt something?"

"Yes, dammit, my mellow state. In case it escaped you, it's my fucking day off. Lucky for you, I can't reach through the phone."

"Wow, you are stressed. I understand. This place is heart attack city, with everyone racing around 24/7 until they collapse. There's no way to keep pace with the growing caseload."

"Okay, Derek, describing how bad things are at work is not helping. Tell me why you're calling."

"An anonymous tip came in at 3 a.m. that Mattie Powell was killed because she refused to help William 'Little Billy' Wilson die. The male caller claimed Powell refused to assist with his suicide. Instead, she offered mental health care counseling."

Oh shit, thought Smith. Was Martha Powell the angel of mercy?

"Did the caller say where to find this Little Billy?"

"They said he could be hiding at his mom's place in Back of the Yards or at Lazy Acres, where he's been living."

"Do you have an address for his mother?"

"Yeah. You enjoy your day off. I'll go check it out. I'll let you know what I find."

"Derek, I'll come to get you at the station, and we'll go together. If this guy is the killer, he might panic when you show up on Mom's doorstep unannounced. See you in an hour."

"Babe," I gotta go," Shondra told Ingrid. "I'll try to get home early for dinner."

"I heard. Do your thing. Don't worry about dinner. If it works out, great. No pressure."

"I love you," she said. They hugged, and then Shonda ran for the shower.

DETECTIVE SMITH CALLED Derek and said she would pick him up in front of the police station.

When she arrived, he was wearing a bulletproof vest under his sports jacket.

"Good thinking," she said, poking his ribs when he got into her car. "Mine is in the trunk."

"What do we know about Willie Wilson?"

"It's William," he corrected her. "I dug out a police report. Detectives Stuart and Lemon interviewed him about a potential perv incident in the shoe department where he had worked."

"Was he arrested?"

"No," said Morton. "The complainant said he looked up her dress while fitting her with shoes."

"What did Lemon and Stuart think?"

"They thought it was a bogus charge, based on inter-views with employees working with Little Billy that day. The complainant went after all the clerks that day about service, prices, then topped it off with the peeping charge. A week later, Wilson was fired."

"I'm not surprised," said Morton. "Companies don't want bad publicity or legal problems, so they're adopting zero-tolerance policies."

"Derek, do you think I'm a woman cop who doesn't know about the *#MeToo* movement?"

"Sorry, boss."

A history buff, Derek looked out the window and pointed to the neighborhood entrance, a stone arch with the engraved words Union Stock - Yard - Chartered - 1865.

"That's all that is left of the Union Stockyard. At its peak, the area was a square mile of livestock pens, slaughter-houses, and processing and packing plants. The annual slaughter was 18 million hogs and cattle.

"Carl Sandberg's poem Chicago may have said it best," said Morton, who recited the first stanza.

Hog Butcher for the World,
Tool Maker, Stacker of Wheat,
Player with Railroads and the Nation's Freight Handler;
Stormy, husky, brawling,
City of the Big Shoulders

"So, Derek, you're a poet *and* a historian?

He ignored her taunt. "In his book *The Jungle*, Upton

Sinclair wrote about the abuses and poor conditions workers suffered in the butchering and processing business. For immigrants from around the world, this was job-central. Nine railroads converged. The ground under the neighborhoods in this area was literally soaked in blood."

"Lovely," said Smith. "Can we save the history and literature lessons until later?"

"I checked on Wilson's mother and found that Anna Wilson's home has been in the family since the rise of this neighborhood," Morton added. "She's likely the descendent of slaughterhouse workers."

"And how is that relevant?"

"The report on the knife came in an hour ago. The blood belongs to the victim. Another set of DNA identified on the handle wasn't in the database. The weapon used was an antique hog butchering knife with the initials MW. A Wilson relative, maybe.

"Damn, you're good," said Smith. "Let's go slow, stay calm, and avoid setting off the suspect if he's here. And let's be ready if he comes out with guns blazing."

"Roger that," said Morton. "Now, put your vest on."

21

Detectives Smith and Morton parked a few doors from Anna Wilson's house in the Back of the Yards neighborhood. The area was tidy, with clean streets and well-maintained houses. The exception was the Wilson home. The grass was weedy. A shutter was askew. The paint had chipped off the faded yellow exterior. Stuffing protruded from a padded chair on the porch. A casual observer might think the owner had abandoned the home.

Smith and Morton walked up four creaky wooden steps and pressed the doorbell. A blaring TV penetrated a cracked window. When no one came to the door, they knocked.

"Get the hell away from my front door. I'm not buying what you're selling."

The woman's voice was the raspy sound of a heavy smoker.

A dog, tiny by the sound of its squeaky voice, yapped in the background.

"Mrs. Wilson, it's Detectives Smith and Morton of the Chicago PD," Smith said.

"What the hell has he done now?" she said.

"Please come out for a moment so we can talk to you."

"Shut the fuck up, you mutt," she yelled.

"Dammit," she said, followed by grunts and groans. "Hold your horses."

A moment later, the door opened, and a woman in a puffy green housecoat with frizzy, unnaturally red hair appeared. A cigarette dangled from lips coated with tangerine lipstick. A bottle of liquor hung from her hand. Her fingernails were cracked and broken.

"I'm here," she slurred, "What do you want?"

"Is your son, William Wilson, home?"

"William? You mean Little Billy. He's a little prick. That ungrateful pervert hasn't been around for a week. He stormed out of here, calling me names as the door slammed behind him. What has he done now?"

"His name has come up in our investigation of Martha Powell's murder."

Wilson laughed.

Smith noticed that the woman didn't ask who Martha Powell was. She either didn't care or remembered the name from the news.

"Little Billy is a loser. He probably did it."

It was the pot calling the kettle black, Smith thought.

"Why do you think he killed her? Did he confess?"

"Hell, no. He's plain mean, considering how he talked to me, his mother. And he owns that knife. I just figured he did it—one more death on his conscience.

"What do you mean by a death on his conscience?" Smith said.

"You should ask him. But when he was a kid, I was a single mother working my ass off to support him and his brother after their good-for-nothing father took off with another woman. Billy's job was looking after his little brother, my dear, perfect Brian. Brian was a beautiful boy. He was two years younger than Billy but a foot taller. The prettiest green eyes you've ever seen. He was smart as a whip. Billy was this tiny, defective thing from day one. I wish he had died in childbirth."

"What happened? Morton said.

"Billy let Brian get hit by a car. My perfect boy was dead at age 10. All because Little fucking Billy didn't watch over him."

A tear stained the woman's puffy, makeup-coated cheek, the first sign of humanity in a mother filled with hate for her son. She took a deep drag from her cigarette, gulped some whiskey, and closed her eyes. She remained that way for a full minute.

Smith didn't ask Anna Wilson where she was when Brian was killed or what role she played because of her life choices. She wasn't a life coach or family counselor. Sometimes, she wanted to shake people and tell them to straighten up and move on with their lives.

"Do you know where we could find Billy?" Smith said.

"Probably down at that damn camp for homeless losers like him."

"Does Billy own a knife?" Smith said.

"He's got an old butcher knife from my grandfather Martin Wilson. Grandpa worked in a slaughterhouse. My daddy worked in a meat packing plant. And I followed Daddy and worked in a hog processing plant. The knife was passed from generation to generation. A nice souvenir, Billy said. I told Billy it wasn't a damn souvenir. It was a piece of family history. I said he couldn't have it unless he continued in the family business. He took it anyway."

"The family business?" Smith said.

"The meat butchering business. Billy said he wasn't interested. I told him that if it was good enough work for us, it was good enough for him. He said he was going better himself. For a start, he said he planned to sell women's shoes. A perfect job for a little pussy."

"We found a knife at the murder scene. It had a hog engraving and the initials MW."

"That's Billy's knife, handed down from old granddad Martin Wilson."

"Is the knife here in the house?" Morton asked.

"I have no idea where it is. Ask Billy—if he ever turns up."

"Where can we find him? "

"Ain't it your job to track him down? He called me a bitch and a whore as he stormed out. Didn't stop to say where he was heading."

Smith wanted to say she agreed with Little Billy's assessment of his mother. Instead, she clenched her jaw and said nothing.

"We'll follow up," Smith said. She felt Anna Wilson would gladly give up her son's location if she knew.

"Better do more than that," she said. "The gun I had is missing. I imagine he's armed and dangerous."

"What kind of gun?"

"Ruger .22 LR," said Wilson. "Small, light, and accurate. Fits nicely in a pocket or handbag."

"Is it registered?"

"Damn right, it is. Got it from a local gun store for protection."

Morton made a note.

"The knife is gone, too. It was a damn good knife. I skinned and deboned a lot of squealing pigs. My record was three minutes." She twisted her hand and stabbed the air as if she held a knife.

Smith stepped back, her hand instinctively brushing her gun. She looked at Morton and shook her head.

"If you hear from William, please call me," said Smith, handing Wilson her card.

"I told you, it ain't William; it's Little Billy, the prick pervert."

They thanked Wilson and left her standing on the porch. When they returned to their car, Smith said, "What a pleasant woman. How would you like a mother like that?" Morton grimaced his mouth a tight line.

"Now we have a suspect possibly armed with the murder weapon and a gun, she said. "You issue a BOLO; we need to get the troops on the lookout for this guy."

"Will do, boss."

"Looks like we've narrowed down the suspect list," said Morton.

"I think the greedy husband is desperate, but I don't see him as a killer," said Smith. "I want to add one more suspect to the list."

Morton looked at her and cocked his head.

"Anna Wilson. She knows her way around a knife and a gun and hates her son. Could have killed Powell to frame her son, hoping to get rid of him."

"That's a stretch," said Morton. "I need to be convinced."

"Let's find Little Billy. Maybe he'll confess or tell us why his mother could have killed Mattie Powell."

Smith's phone vibrated.

"It's Chief Blackburn," she said.

"Yeah, boss."

"You're kidding me. I thought this *was* our top priority."

She hung up and said, "Blackburn just yanked us from the case. Says something with higher priority has come up."

22

"I don't get it," said Jenny Morrison. "Police were swarming the death of Mattie Powell because of her celebrity status as a best-selling author. "I just got off the phone with Detective Smith. She and Detective Morton have been assigned to another case. She assured me that it's temporary, that the investigation will continue but couldn't tell me when."

"Guess we're on our own," said Briggs. "We need to get people talking down at Lazy Acres. Someone knows someone who knows something. The place is a beehive of gossip."

"Remember Bobbie-Jean Worth, the woman with the beagle-basset mix?"

"She's the queen bee of gossip," he said. "Confide in her and it goes viral."

"That could work for us," said Jenny. "We'll tell her we need help finding Mattie's killer. Lazy Acres will be abuzz by nightfall."

"Detective Smith won't like it," said Briggs. "But Mattie's murder demands desperate measures."

Their plan was simple. Jenny would visit Bobbie-Jean and tell her Dr. Jim was back and needed her help. When she had information to share with Briggs, she would put a lantern in front of her tent. That was the signal when a Lazy Acres resident wanted him to check out a dog.

"After surgery this morning, I'll go see Bobbie-Jean and stir up the hive."

"Don't get stung," he said, giving her a light, playful pinch. She kissed him and said, "I'll be sure to wear my beekeeper suit."

JIM BRIGGS COULDN'T BELIEVE he was back in Chicago, strolling the main street of Lazy Acres. The sweet smell of Forest Park, Portland's giant urban forest, surrounded him at home. Here, smoke from wildfires in Canada and the usual big-city stink from cars, trucks, and trash choked the air. By contrast, he had always liked Chicago's clean-smelling foggy nights when he could disappear into the mist as he wandered from tent to tent, doctoring the dogs of the unsheltered.

His first stop was Bobbie-Jean Worth's home. Saying she lived in a tent—singular—was a joke since she had collected multiple shelters over a decade and cobbled together what she called her castle—more like a well-furnished two-bedroom apartment with canvas walls.

As planned, a lantern out front signaled the gossip fest was about to begin. Arriving at Worth's compound, Briggs called out.

"Dr. Jim, I've been waiting for you," she said. A second later, a big woman with rosy cheeks, frizzy black hair, and green eyes burst out of the tent and hugged Briggs. At 6 feet

6, hugs were usually around Briggs' waist. Hers were chest high. He hugged her back.

"Bobbie-Jean, let me look at you. You're a sweet treat for the eyes, as always."

"Dr. Jim, you're quite the hunk yourself." Briggs blushed.

"Sorry you lost your friend, Mattie," said Briggs.

"A horrible thing," she said. "I miss her so much."

"Me, too," said Briggs. "Mattie and I were best friends. We worked as a team to help people in the community."

"She told me she loved your connection and admired you for never taking advantage, let alone a dollar, to help people here." Briggs smiled.

"I know Jenny told you we've been working with the police to find her killer. Yesterday, we discovered the detectives on the case have been reassigned to another investigation. It looks like it's up to us to find the killer and turn them over to the police."

"Come in," she said. "Let me tell you what I know."

Over the next hour, she fed Briggs community members theories, fantasies, and anecdotes. Finally, she revealed the consensus, fingering Little Billy Wilson as the killer.

One unnamed source told her he had spotted Little Billy at an AA meeting where he had met a woman he was now shacking up with. Their 'shack' was a nearly abandoned terminal at Chicago Midway Airport. That was before she snagged a government-subsidized apartment less than a mile from Lazy Acres. Bobbie-Jean provided the address.

Armed with intel on Little Billy, he examined Bobbie Jean's dog, Pepper, and declared the hound healthy. Briggs hugged and thanked the woman. He was always surprised at how good she smelled, like fresh-cut roses.

Exiting the tent, Briggs started toward home. He felt certain Little Billy was the killer. It made sense. Now, he and

Jenny had to verify the man's whereabouts and give it to the police. He texted Jenny 'leaving now' after climbing out of Bobbie-Jean's tent.

He shouldered his medical bag, put his phone in his pocket, and then began walking. He had taken a dozen steps when a shadowy figure emerged from the mist. He stopped. Squinting, he tried to bring the image into focus. Someone on the small side, he thought. A hand extended toward him. "Bastard," the figure yelled, followed by a gunshot.

Briggs grabbed his chest and went down.

23

Little Billy Wilson waited until dark before approaching his mother's house.

He wanted his clothes, a Gibson guitar he learned to play as a boy, and a photo of his dead brother, Brian. To get them, he was ready to battle with his mother, Anna Wilson—one more time. She likely would be drunk and passed out with a half-smoked cigarette burning in an ashtray. The furniture, carpets, and counters had all suffered burns from leaving cigarettes unattended. How hard would it be, he wondered, to use a gloved hand to push an ashtray with a lit cigarette onto the carpet and leave? A fitting end, he thought, for an inhuman person who wanted him dead.

Mother and son were biologically connected, but she was dead to him otherwise. Anna Wilson would register as a flatline if they hooked Billy up to a brain wave monitor to measure his feelings for her, the result of a lifetime of physical and mental abuse.

Billy never understood why she had blamed him for Brian's death. One day, they were riding their bikes home from school when Brian yelled, 'Let's go,' and took off like a shot. It was a game of who could be first at the next stop sign, intersection, or driveway. Innocent child's play.

Brian was bigger, stronger, and had longer legs, even though he was two years younger. He inherited his father's genes rather than his mother's petiteness. His physical advantages helped him win eight out of 10 of their bike races. Rainy days were their favorites, jockeying for position to see who could hit puddles hardest and kick up the most water on each other.

It was a sunny day when Brian launched a race to the corner. Only this time, he didn't stop. He raced through a stoplight, raised his hands declaring victory, and looked behind him to see Little Billy's reaction.

At that exact moment, a driver blew his horn. Brian looked up, his face a horror mask. The oncoming car, traveling the speed limit, hit him broadside. The helmetless Brian and the bike flew 50 feet in the air, and he came crashing down on his head. He died in the emergency department.

When the ED doctor gave her the news, Mrs. Wilson hit him in the face and began smashing anything she could put her hands on. It took four security guards to subdue her. After injecting her with a sedative, a psychiatrist on duty committed her to the hospital's psychiatric ward for evaluation. She was transferred to a psychiatric hospital, where she remained for six months; the first month, she was catatonic.

Billy's Aunt Mary cared for him in his mother's absence and was kind and supportive. The opposite of Anna. She apologized for her sister's behavior and almost convinced him that the accident wasn't his fault. He still felt guilty because he was the big brother, and his mother had repeatedly told him it was his job to look after Brian. Why hadn't he listened?

After returning home, Anna was a zombie from drugs given to her for depression, anxiety, and insomnia. When she wasn't sleeping or drinking, she screamed at Billy for 'killing my Brian.'

Like a scrapbooker gone wild, she had plastered the house with photos of Brian playing Little League, holding up his merit badges from Boy Scouts, or mugging in school pictures. Thumb tacks held hundreds of photos to the living room, kitchen, and hallway walls.

None of the photos included Little Billy. His mother took a pair of scissors to the only portrait of the two of them—brothers in arms. A severed hand, eerily draped over Brian's shoulder, was the only visual evidence of their bond.

Despite extensive therapy, for most of his life, Billy had suffered guilt for the sin his mother accused him of—dereliction of duty to guard his younger sibling's life. It wasn't until Billy turned 21 that something clicked in his brain, telling him that his mother felt guilty for not schooling the boys on traffic safety or coming to pick them up from school. She blamed herself for the accident but took it out on Little Billy, smothering him with her grief.

Why he remained living at home, taking her constant abuse—including belittling him in front of his few girlfriends—was beyond him. The only possible reason, he thought, was that his weekly paychecks kept her supplied with liquor and cigarettes, helped with the rent, and paid the utilities. Occasionally, when he brought home groceries, Camels, and bourbon, she would thank him and say he was a good boy. In those rare moments, Billy would go to his room and sob. A crust of love was better than nothing. His world seemed brighter until she ignited her verbal blow-torch and scolded him for being a loser the next day.

Finally, he had moved on, escaped Lazy Acres, entered AA, and found a new girlfriend. They were living together in her rent-subsidized studio apartment. He shared the cost, using savings from his shoe salesman job. Now, he was waiting for a sales job at an independent clothing store. He was honest with the owner about his firing but supplied the woman with the final police report, which included inter-views with people he had worked with and the detective's conclusion that he did nothing wrong.

He pulled a key from his pocket and slipped quietly through the backdoor. There were no lights or TV blaring, so he assumed his mother was out drinking at one of her local dive bars. He knew every inch of the place, so there was no need for a light.

He entered his room and filled a duffel bag with keep-sakes and hidden cash. Billy looked around, then walked to the living room where the familiar stench of body odor, smoke, and spilled bourbon infected the air. As he turned to leave, a key rattled in the front door lock. A second later, Anna pushed her way in and fumbled for the light switch. Barely able to stand, she focused on Billy.

"Well, well, the worthless little shit has returned."

Looking at his duffel bag, she said, "What are you stealing?"

"I'm taking what's mine. They can bury you with the rest of this shit. I'm never returning."

"No," she said. "You won't be returning. The only place you'll be going is prison."

Billy looked at her.

"Got nothing to say, huh? That's okay. The cops are going to be on your tiny ass any minute. I got that damn veterinarian good," she said, whooping and wobbling before falling into her overstuffed chair.

"What the hell did you do?"

"I killed that angel of mercy man. Shot him in the heart. When his head hit the concrete, it cracked like an egg. Lucky for him, he never knew what hit him."

"Oh my god, you killed Jim Briggs?"

"Deader than a cockroach smashed with a hammer."

"You're going to Hell," said Little Billy.

"Yeah, well, that's between the Good Lord and me. I think he'll see it my way."

"If not Hell, you'll go to jail for sure." Billy started to dial 9-1-1.

"Good luck with that," said Anna. "You're the one who will get strung you up for it. When two detectives came looking for you, I told them you stole my gun and granddaddy's pig knife. Oh yeah, Little Prick Billy, your ass is fried. You'll go down for two murders. I'll be rid of you once and for all. You'll finally pay for what you did to my perfect little boy, Brian. Now, get your ass out of my house."

Little Billy was stunned. He closed his phone, turned, and walked out.

Standing in his backyard, he shook his head and said to no one, "My mother framed me for murder. What did I do to deserve that?"

Now, he had a new problem: a bounty on his head. The police could be storming his and Rebecca's apartment at any moment. They both could die in a hail of gunfire because of his mother's murderous behavior and lies.

He got on his phone and dialed Rebecca. "Sweetheart. Trust what I'm about to say. There's no time to waste."

"What are you talking about?"

"My mother told the police I killed a man and am armed with a gun she claims I stole from her. We need to run for it, or we'll both be killed. Get packed. I'll be there in a few minutes, and we'll head for the airport. I have money for tickets. We'll go to Mexico and start over."

24

B obbie-Jean Worth heard a loud pop.

She opened her tent and stepped out. Moving tentatively with her lantern light leading the way, she moved toward a dark mass on the ground.

"Oh, my god," she yelled. "Dr. Jim has been shot."

She ran to Briggs' side and saw blood spreading across his chest and coming from an ear. She screamed, setting off her Beagle-Basset Pepper's piercing howl.

Heads and bodies flew out of tents and ran toward her.

Mel Brockman, Bobbie-Jean's nearest neighbor, was first to come to her aide. Sobbing, she pointed to Briggs' inert body. He took one look and dialed 9-1-1.

"Anyone know basic first aid?"

"I was an LVN and saw plenty of slit wrists among nursing home residents looking for a way out," said Edna Phillips.

"Do your thing," Brockman said.

Phillips responded, using a scarf to apply pressure to the chest wound.

"Tell me the nature of your emergency," the 9-1-1 operator said, more relaxed than you would expect. The operators were trained to be calm. This woman sounded as if she was about to take a nap. No doubt, she knew the origin of the call was Lazy Acres and suspected it was a crank call.

Brockman, a former accountant who lost his family, business, and home to alcoholism, was still good at details.

"This is Melvin Brockman, a resident of the Lazy Acres community. I'm reporting a shooting. The victim is James Allen Briggs, a veterinarian at Paws Care Emergency Hospital. He provides care to the dogs in our homeless community. It appears he has suffered a gunshot wound in the chest and a head injury. He needs emergency medical treatment."

"Standby," the operator said. "I'm dispatching help. I have locked onto your phone location, so please stay where you are. And leave your phone turned on. Police and paramedics are on the way. Apply pressure to his wounds as quickly as possible to slow the bleeding. Is the shooter still in the area?"

"The shooter appears to have gone," he said. "I've got a woman here helping with the first aid."

He hung up and said, "Let's get something under his head. Until the paramedics arrive, we're his lifeline."

While they waited for the cavalry to arrive, Brockman asked if anyone had Jenny Morrison's phone number. A half dozen neighbors raised their hands.

"Give it to me," Brockman said.

When Jenny picked up, Brockman identified himself. "Dr. Morrison, Dr. Jim has been shot. I called 9-1-1, and they are sending help. He's not conscious. I can't tell how badly he's injured. He appears to have chest and head wounds.

"Tell them to take Dr. Briggs to UCMC, the University of Chicago Medical Center. I'll meet them there."

"Will do," said Brockman. "I'll stand by so you can talk to the paramedics."

Another two minutes went by before sirens filled the air.

SWAT members swarmed, guns drawn, heads swiveling, looking for the shooter.

Satisfied the area was clear, they allowed paramedics in. When they arrived, Brockman identified Briggs and said, "I have his doctor on the line. She wants him to go to UCMC for care. She'll meet you there."

A paramedic got on Brockman's phone, talked to Jenny, and agreed to her request.

"Let's get him on board and get out of here," the paramedic said. Police cleared the way for the ambulance to exit, pushing back a crowd of more than 100 homeless people. Usually, when police appeared, they pulled back into their homes like cockroaches scurrying to safety. Not today. When one of their own was in trouble, they never failed to come to the rescue. And they considered Dr. Jim one of their own.

"Let the ambulance and police escort get by," Brockman yelled. The crowd moved quickly out of the way.

A cop approached Brockman, who still had Jenny on his line.

"Officer, Dr. Briggs's colleague, Jenny Morrison, is standing by to speak with you."

The officer identified himself as Mike Jameson.

"Officer Jameson, please contact homicide Detective Shondra Smith. She's investigating the death of Mattie Powell, the best-selling author killed at Lazy Acres. I'm certain this shooting is related, so she'll want to know immediately. The murder suspect is on the loose."

"Roger, that," said Jameson. He handed the phone back to Brockman.

"Everyone believes Mattie's murder is the work of Little Billy Wilson," said Brockman. "I think Billy shot Dr. Jim."

"We'll get him," Jenny said. "Thanks for your help."

25

T he paramedic ambulance roared up to the entrance of the UCMC emergency room, setting off a rush of doctors and nurses, ready to meet their latest gunshot victim.

Because of Briggs' size—6 feet 6 and 225 pounds—a half dozen people were needed to transfer him from the gurney to a treatment table.

"The patient is James Allen Briggs, a Paws Care Emergency Hospital veterinary surgeon," a paramedic said. "He's the vet for Lazy Acres, where we picked him up."

ER Physician Mary Bidwell looked up and cocked her head. "They have money for pet care?"

"Briggs does it as a community service." Dr. Bidwell nodded.

"Alert neurosurgery," she said. "Possible skull fracture. We need a head CT scan, STAT."

A nurse cut off Briggs's shirt, exposing a shattered stethoscope. Dr. Bidwell picked it up, looked at a hole in the middle, and examined the wound.

"This is Briggs' lucky day," said Dr. Bidwell. "His stethoscope absorbed most of the bullet energy." She examined the wound with her gloved hand, picked up forceps, pushed it gently under the skin, and pulled out a bullet fragment.

"It is a .22 caliber, so it didn't break through the chest wall." UCMC got its share of the city's 2,000 annual shootings, making the ER a master class on ballistics.

After his chest wound was closed, Briggs was transferred to the neurosurgery unit for a craniotomy to relieve pressure on his brain.

Dr. Bidwell walked to the waiting room three hours later to update Briggs' family. She called out Briggs' name and saw a woman she vaguely recognized come forward.

"I'm Jenny Morrison, Jim Briggs' colleague," she said. "I'm also his girlfriend and his only family."

"Small world," said Bidwell. "You probably won't remember this, but five years ago, you operated on my dog after a car hit him. You saved his life."

Momentarily distracted by the memory, Morrison said, "I remember you and your standard poodle. It was touch and go, but she was a tough girl. I'm so glad she made it."

"Yes, and she's still going strong. But you're not here for a reunion. Dr. Briggs suffered a fractured skull and a brain bleed, which our neurosurgeon team has relieved. They've induced a coma to help with his recovery."

Jenny Grimaced. Her patients were dogs, but she knew about head injuries and possible outcomes. She had performed numerous canine craniotomies.

"It's wait and see," said Bidwell. "There's some good news. His stethoscope slowed the bullet. It lodged in his left pectoral muscle, which I removed. It should heal with no problem."

Jenny let out a sigh of relief and hugged Bidwell. Tears filled her eyes.

"Thank you," said Jenny.

"We should know soon about the head trauma," said Bidwell.

"In the meantime, you can visit him, assuming the cop guarding the door will let you pass."

JENNY MORRISON WENT to the CCU, where an armed uniformed officer guarded Briggs' room.

"I'm his colleague," she explained.

"Sorry, I can't let anyone in," he said coldly.

"It's okay, a voice called from behind her." The cop nodded and moved aside.

Morrison looked around. It was Detective Smith.

"Go ahead and go in."

"He wouldn't be here, comatose with a bullet wound and fractured skull if you had done your job and had stayed on the case like the Mayor promised the public."

"I had no choice; I got pulled. As a result of the shooting, my boss has put me back on the case."

"The word on the street at Lazy Acres is that Little Billy Wilson killed Mattie and no doubt shot Jimmy," said Jenny.

"We've got the same information and are trying to track down Wilson. Detective Morton is checking out a lead on a suspected location."

"I'm sorry about Dr. Briggs. We'll get Wilson. In the meantime, I'll let you get on with your visit."

"You better before someone else gets killed," said Jenny, a scowl on her face. "I don't need regrets. I need action. This is your fault.

Detective Smith stared at the receding woman, her jaw grinding.

Jenny entered the room, looked at the man who could be her husband and the father of her children, and burst into tears. Her shoulders shook with grief and anger. She wanted to wrap this man up and protect him from all the bad things in the world. And she wanted to punch him for his carelessness. Maybe he was here because he cared too much.

"You should have stayed in Portland," she told the comatose Briggs. "I'm not worth the trouble. I love you. I want you to be in my life. But the time isn't right." She held and caressed his hand, then kissed him.

An incoming call snapped her to attention. The caller was Rob Merritt. She walked into the hallway outside Briggs's room and answered.

"Rob, Jim's been shot. He's in the hospital with a chest wound and a fractured skull. He's in a coma."

"Oh no," he said. "What's his condition."

"It's grave," said Jenny, tears starting to flow again.

"Who did this?" said Merritt, angry someone would hurt his friend and savior. "Did they catch the guy?"

"No, but the word at Lazy Acres is that Little Billy Wilson killed Mattie and shot Jim, trying to get rid of both for not euthanizing him. Saying the words make me numb."

"I was calling to tell you my investigator has located Wilson and his girlfriend, Rebecca. He has left the information on the police tip hotline. The cops should be moving on it immediately."

"Rob, that's good news," she said. "I chewed out the detective for dropping the murder investigation for another case. Now she's back full-time, looking for Mattie's killer and Jim's assailant. I'm not sure I believe her."

"Why was Jim at Lazy Acres?"

"We had asked Bobby-Jean Worth to tell her gossip network that the cops had let down the community again, pulling out of Mattie's investigation. Jim went to see what she had come up with."

Jenny told Rob about the shooting, the stethoscope deflecting much of the bullet, and possible outcomes for the head injury.

"I'll pray for his recovery," said Rob.

"Thanks," said Jenny.

"One more thing. I have a private jet to transport you and your dad to Portland if you decide to go. There would be a doctor aboard. When you arrive, I'll have medical specialists lined up for you to interview. You and Jim could be together and take care of Dad." Jenny sighed.

"Rob, I should call you the angel of mercy. Jim and I will discuss it when he recovers."

"Consider me your genie, who won't limit you to three wishes."

"I like that," said Jenny, her voice suddenly lighter.

They hung up, and Jenny returned to Brigg's room.

"Jimmy, could we move Dad to Oregon and have a life while still caring for him in his final days?" The only answer was the monitor's sound measuring his heart rate and breathing. She sensed that the beat increased just the slightest bit.

Could he hear her? Was that a yes to being together in Portland?

She would find out if Briggs woke up.

26

Detectives Smith and Morton looked at the map. The location of Little Billy's apartment, his mother's home, and Lazy Acres formed a loose triangle.

"The unidentified source on the tip line gave us his address and noted that he also attends Alcoholics Anonymous here," said Morton, pointing to a church near the apartment. "I checked, and AA meetings are held on Thursday evenings."

"Good work, Morton," said Smith. "I've already got SWAT on high alert. Let's saddle up. We need to get this guy before he hurts someone else."

Smith picked up the line and dialed SWAT Commander Elliott Pearson.

"Ready to go?" Pearson said.

"Yep," said Smith. "Just a reminder. The guy reportedly stole his mother's .22 caliber pistol and may have shot at least one man who is in the hospital with chest and head wounds. He could have panicked and armored up. As far as his record goes, he's Snow White. He never had a traffic ticket. But desperate men do desperate things. You know the drill: we'll be on high alert."

"Roger that," said Pearson. "I'll have the troops locked and loaded in 15 minutes and lined up for your lead."

"See you at the back lot," she said and hung up.

After she and Morton checked their weapons in the trunk and climbed into bulletproof vests, Smith led the team, in precision formation, to Windy City Apartments. Daytime raids were risky to police and civilians. But they needed to get Little Billy in custody ASAP.

When they arrived at the building, children played in a swimming pool. Bystanders were everywhere.

Rather than cause a panic, Smith signed for her team to hold back, opened the gate, and walked in. She smiled and walked around the pool, signaling everyone to move toward the entry gate where armed officers were waiting. She put her finger to her lips, asking them to go quietly.

Once the area was cleared, the officers moved upstairs to the second floor, approaching the target apartment from two directions.

Standing to the side of the door, Smith knocked and identified herself. She shook her head, indicating there was no response, and gave a hand signal that it was time to enter.

A SWAT member moved up with a battering ram and smashed open the door. He moved aside and let the armed team swarm the one-bedroom apartment.

"All clear," Elliot Pearce spoke into his mic.

"Damn, I don't know what happened," said Smith. "The intel looked solid."

As they walked downstairs, a woman who had been at the pool walked up to Smith and Pearce. "If you're looking for Little Billy and Rebecca, they hurried out of here about 30 minutes ago, the woman said. They seemed to be in a hurry."

"Do you know where they went?" said Smith.

"I have no idea," she said. "They were real nice folks. Never caused any trouble."

"Thanks," said Smith.

"Don't worry about it," said Commander Pearce. "The team needs missions to stay sharp. We'll be ready when you get a new line on this guy."

Smith gave Pearce a playful tap on the shoulder.

Smith and Pearce were old friends, working as partners in patrol for a year.

"Elliot, you know that steak place you like?"

"Gibsons Bar and Steakhouse."

"To celebrate, after we lock this perp down, I'm going to treat you to the biggest damn steak you've ever eaten."

"Shondra, don't bullshit me. You know how much I like my steak. We're talking $82 for a 22-ounce ribeye at Gibson's, plus a pre-dinner martini and some good cabernet sauvignon to wash down the steak. And cab fare."

"I'm figuring $300 for us both. I've been saving," said Shondra. "Can't think of anybody else I would like to celebrate my ten years in the department."

"Damn, then it's my anniversary, too," he said. "How could I forget we were rookies together? That was ages ago. Only ten years?"

"You've got a deal, Shondra. Good luck tracking down this Little Billy character. When you ready to take him down, let me know."

"I'll issue an APB and get the ground troops looking for him. He can't be far. We'll get him and lock up his ass."

"Give'em hell, girl," said Pearce.

"You know I will," she said.

LITTLE BILLY and Rebecca had escaped the apartment to the church, where they met and attended AA meetings. A separate building off the church parking lot provided a refuge for people on the run or for those who just needed a place for a short rest. No questions asked. No judgment.

After dropping off Rebecca, Little Billy headed back to the apartment.

He suspected the police were coming for him after what his mother said. He knew she was mostly hot air. Yet, there was something odd about her this time; he thought she had finally slipped a gear, crazed.

She repeatedly said she hated him, but would she frame him for murder? Had she shot Jim Briggs? Could she have killed Mattie, angry because she wouldn't kill him? He needed to find out if the police were coming for him. So, he hid across the street to watch. He would expect one or two detectives to knock on the door if they came. A minute later, carloads of cops pulled up to the apartment building.

Billy was panicked, his pulse pounding as he watched the scene unfold. What if he had been inside his apartment, oblivious to the raid? He likely would have been killed in the onslaught.

When he saw his neighbors cleared out of the pool area and cops smashing in his door, followed by a full SWAT assault, he knew his mother hadn't lied. He was in big trouble. After the police cleared out, he returned to the church.

"Becky," he whispered. "We've got to get out of here. We'll go to the airport, and buy a ticket for Mexico. I've got enough money in the bank to support us for six months while we find jobs. I've been there before. We'll figure it out. But we will have a roof over our heads, good weather, and good food."

"Why not," she said. "I've got no one here and no reason to stay."

27

L ittle Billy and Rebecca hunkered down in Chicago O'Hare Airport's Terminal 2, which had once housed Delta Airlines. With Delta's move to a new location, the lack of foot traffic created a respite for the unsheltered. Toilets, water, coffee, and food, including the bits thrown in the trash by rushed travelers, created a warm, safe environment.

With Rebecca safe from arrest, Little Billy put on his cap to block security camera facial recognition and walked to the counter at Mexicana Airlines. He bought two coach tickets to Ixtapa, a Mexican Riviera resort area. The flight was scheduled to depart in four hours, at 9:45 pm.

He returned to Terminal 2, sat beside Rebecca, and gave her the flight information. "We'll fly into Ixtapa, take a vacation, then find a job at a resort. We'll look for an apartment in Zihuatanejo, a small fishing village nearby.

"Won't the cops track us down and have us deported?" Rebecca said.

"Of course, they could. I'm betting they will discover I had nothing to do with the two murders my mother committed. She's too stupid to keep her mouth shut. She'll brag about how she set me up. We'll be free and clear."

"Let's hope so," she said. "I'm scared."

He hugged her. "I've got you. We'll be fine. We'll be free of this city and my mother in a few hours." Rebecca smiled.

"Rebecca, let's clean up, and I'll buy breakfast. Afterward, we'll move into the International terminal and lose ourselves in the crush of flyers."

28

R ob Merritt's private investigator, Mike Martin, had followed Little Billy to the airport, disguising himself as a homeless man staying close to his target.

Martin followed them to the International terminal. After they settled at a gate, he texted their description and exact location to Shondra Smith.

"Who's this?" she wrote back.

"A friend hired to find Little Billy Wilson. You and I have met. Names don't matter. You want this guy. No way to tell if he's armed. BTW, he's wearing a navy blue knit hat with a Chicago Bears logo."

Smith texted a thumbs up.

Martin kept an eye on the couple while he waited for police to arrive. It wasn't long.

They crept from two different locations, trying to avoid a shootout without bystanders getting hurt. Since the flight was several hours away, they lucked out. The gate was nearly empty.

All at once, heavily armed Chicago Police and airport

security flooded the area, screaming for Little Billy and Rebecca to get down. A dozen guns pointed at their heads. Two cops frisked and handcuffed them while another searched their bags for weapons.

The response team leader walked over to Smith, who had just arrived. "All is secure. No sign of weapons. Just two tickets to Mexico."

Smith thanked him and walked over to Little Billy.

"I'm innocent," Little Billy squeaked. "My mother set me up. She killed Mattie and Dr. Briggs."

"Dr. Briggs is alive," said Detective Smith. "You'll have a chance to tell your story when we get downtown."

"At least, you should release Rebecca. She had nothing to do with any of this. We just met."

"Rebecca is a witness," said Smith.

With Little Billy and his girlfriend secured, she thanked her team and the airport cops.

"Morton and I will take it from here," she said.

Her phone buzzed. She looked down at a text and turned around.

"Iron Butt Mike Martin. Is that you?"

"The one and only."

"You were the anonymous caller leaving clues on our tip line?"

"Might have been?" he said, grinning broadly.

They hugged.

Martin had been one of her training officers when she was a rookie. The man saved her life at least once. Burned out on policing after a dozen years as a street cop, he went private.

"Who's your sugar daddy on this case?" Shonda said.

"Shondra, you know I never kiss and tell."

She laughed.

"But you can take me out for beer and pizza after you close the murder book on the Powell killing."

"You got it," she said. "Now that I have Little Billy in custody, I can wrap it up quickly. Assuming Jim Briggs doesn't die."

"That's all you need to screw up the works," said Martin. "What was all that stuff about his mother setting him up?"

"After meeting his mother, who clearly hates him, Billy may be right about her trying to get rid of him."

"What a shit show," said Martin. "Good luck."

29

Police had separated Rebecca Smart and Little Billy Wilson for their interviews.

Detective Smith would interview Little Billy, while her partner, Derek Morton, would question Rebecca.

Little Billy sat chained to the table in the interview room. He had coffee in front of him, and the room was a comfortable temperature. After 10 minutes, Detective Smith entered and asked him if he needed anything else before starting.

"Take off cuffs," he said, holding up his hands."

She nodded at a uniformed officer standing near the door. He came over and removed the chains.

"Thanks," he said, rubbing his wrists. "I won't be here long. I'm innocent, and I can prove it."

"Of course," Smith said. "We'll get to that."

She read him his rights, which he waived, and gave her permission to record the interview.

"Why were you leaving the country?" she said.

"I didn't want to get caught for something I didn't do. My mother lied and made me look like Mattie Powell's killer."

"Why would she do that?"

"She hates me."

Smith knew why but wanted to hear it from Little Billy.

"She blamed me for my brother's death when we were kids. He rode his bike into traffic and was hit and killed by a car. I was supposed to be watching him. The truth is, he was a wild child and a lot bigger than me. We were kids, always horsing around on our bikes. Thinking I could have prevented the accident is absurd. Still, I've felt guilty most of my life, and she never let me forget that I let her and Brian down and got him killed."

"You want me to believe your mother has been pissed at you for 40 years for something that wasn't your fault"?

"Detective, get my phone. Please. There's a recording of my mother confessing it was a setup."

"Is that so?"

"Yes, I made it yesterday when I went to her house to pick up some personal things for our trip to Mexico. She walked in while I was there and began berating me. She said she would be ridding the world of me for good after taking care of Jim Briggs. Then she pulled out her gun and waved it around. She threatened to shoot me if I didn't leave. 'I'll kill you just like I killed that dog doctor, she said."

"Your mother says you stole the gun and the knife found at the scene of Mattie Powell's murder."

Little Billy's head dropped toward his lap. He looked defeated.

"Okay, Detective, I can see where this is going. Time for a confession."

Smith sat up, checked her tape recorder, and locked her eyes on Little Billy.

"Go on," she said.

"The truth is, after a customer accused me of looking up

her dress while she was trying on shoes, I was fired. Despite being cleared by your department, my mother called me a pervert and continued her punishing diatribe. I fell into a funk and decided to move out and into Lazy Acres. I started drinking heavily."

"How is this related to the murder of Mattie Powell and the Jim Briggs shooting?"

"I'm coming to that. I wanted to die. I heard that a local veterinarian, known as the Angel of Mercy, would inject you on request with the killing drugs he to euthanize dogs."

"Who was the veterinarian?" said Smith.

"Jim Briggs. Anyone who wanted Dr. Briggs to send them onto the next world would first go through Mattie Powell. She told me no. Said I needed mental health counseling, not death. I insisted on meeting Briggs. When we finally talked, he said he agreed with Mattie. I was infuriated. I wanted them both dead. And I think I told my mother that."

"That's quite a tale, Billy."

Smith tried to remain calm. Little Billy had just confirmed her suspicions about Briggs. All she needed now were the names of the murder victims to pin on the good doctor.

"It's true," said Little Billy. "Please check my phone for the recording of my mother." He gave Smith his unlock code and insisted on terminating the interview until she had listened to his mother's confession.

Smith got up, turned off the recorder, and left the room.

Waiting for her outside was Detective Morton.

They shared the stories they got from each suspect. The details matched.

"I think Rebecca Smart is telling the truth," said Morton. "Little Billy's mom *is* a monster. She wants her boy dead. She would do anything to get rid of him. We witnessed her hatred for Billy first-hand.

Smith went to the evidence box on her desk, pulled out Little Billy's phone, punched in the unlock code, and played his messages.

"Morton, listen to this."

"It's the proverbial smoking gun," he said.

"Let's line up Elliot Pearce's team. We're going to move on Mother Wilson. We know she is armed and capable of anything, so we will move after dark."

30

D etective Smith pulled SWAT Commander Elliot Pearce aside to discuss the assault on Anna Wilson.

"Elliot, we interviewed this woman a week ago. She is vile; she hates her son and wants him dead. She blames him for a bicycle accident that killed her youngest son 40 years ago. We have her confession on a phone recording. She said she killed Mattie Powell and tried to kill Jim Briggs to frame her son."

"That's bizarre."

"You think?"

"She had hoped we would kill Billy when we raided his apartment. According to Billy, she is armed and dangerous. We know she owns a pea shooter—a .22-caliber. But we know a.22 kills. She's an experienced knife handler who bragged about slaughtering and skinning a live pig in three minutes at her job in a meat processing plant. Our victim, Mattie Powell, had been stabbed a dozen times with a knife that had belonged to Mrs. Wilson's grandfather."

"Did you find DNA or prints on the knife?"

"We found both. They connect to no one in our databases. However, we know neither Billy nor Mrs. Wilson have a criminal record. Neither had been fingerprinted until we caught Billy at the airport. We've got someone working on the prints."

"Recording her was a smart idea," said Pearce. "What's our next move?"

"Morton and I've discussed it. One option is to return to her home, knock on the door, and tell her we are looking for her son; we ask her if she has any more information about Little Billy's whereabouts. Once she comes to the front door and we can see she isn't armed, we'll ask her to come in and see his room to look for clues. Once inside, we can take her down."

"That's damn risky. What if word has gotten back to her that Billy is already in custody? He could have made a call to her. You could walk into a slaughterhouse."

"The other option is to surround the house at night and do a full assault," Smith said.

"You've heard her confession and are pretty certain she's the killer—and she's armed. A soft approach seems dangerous," he said. "One and done is my recommendation. In and out, lightning fast under the cover of darkness."

"You're right. Let's go for it. Nine tonight. We'll line up a few blocks away, then caravan in."

"One more thing," said Smith. "Mrs. Wilson is a drunk. I suspect she'll be in the bag long before we arrive. If you believe Billy, she passes out by 8 p.m. most nights.

"On the other hand," said Pearce. "She could be using that as a ploy, expecting us to show up thinking she was a helpless old drunk, letting loose with an AK47 she picked up this week."

"Yeah. I know you're right."

Smith walked down the hall to the room where they were holding Billy.

She entered the room and said, "I heard your mother's confession."

"Good, then I can go free."

"Yes, you're free for now. You need to stick around until we have closure on this case."

"I hope you mean when my mother is behind bars."

"Leave that to us," she said. "And you should stay away from your mother's house until we can talk to her."

"I won't ever return to that house."

"Good. You and Rebecca are free to go. Do you have a place to stay?"

"If the apartment manager has repaired the door you smashed, we'll stay there. Rent is paid for another three weeks."

"Detective, if we decide to stay, we'll need a letter from you or your department clearing us. Her clean record was the only way Rebecca could get a rent-subsidized apartment."

"I can arrange that," said Smith. "Sorry for the misunderstanding concerning your role in Mattie Powell's murder and Jim Briggs' shooting."

"Are you saying Jim Briggs is alive?"

"He suffered a fractured skull when he fell after he was shot. He's in a coma. They had to operate to remove blood from his brain. It's not a pretty picture. If he dies, a second murder charge will get added to the Powell killing."

"What the hell was my mother thinking?"

"She wanted you dead."

31

SWAT surrounded Anna Wilson's home in the Back of the Yards neighborhood.

They came in quietly, 20-strong. Fully armed and armored. Team members took up positions in the front and back of the home.

The light from a TV flickered inside, creating an eerie effect on the window shades. An episode of *I Love Lucy* was blaring.

Detectives Smith and Morton stood 20 yards from the front door. "Everyone ready?" she said quietly into her shoulder mic. "We know this woman owns a gun. She may have acquired additional weapons. We believe she is responsible for a murder and an assault with a deadly weapon. She's likely going to be drunk. Remember, I want to take her alive. At the same time, if she points a gun your way, you have permission to shoot her."

"Let's do it," said Pearce.

Smith pulled out a bullhorn and boomed her voice at the tiny house.

"Mrs. Wilson, this is the Chicago Police Department. We

have surrounded your home. Please come out with your hands up."

No response.

"Anna Wilson, members of the Chicago Police Department have surrounded your home. We have a warrant for your arrest."

The TV suddenly went silent. A curtain was pulled back, and a face peered from inside. The front door opened.

"What the hell is going on out there?" a slurred voice said.

Smith repeated her demand and added, "Mrs. Wilson, we met the other day and talked about the death of Mattie Powell. We believe you may have additional information related to our case. We need you to step outside, unarmed, and come to the station to talk to us."

"No fucking way," she said, wobbling as she swigged whiskey from a bottle in her right hand.

"Little Billy is the one you want," she said. "I've got nothing to do with nothing. And I've got nothing to say. Billy can swing."

"We talked to him," Mrs. Wilson said. "Now, we need to speak with you."

"I told you. I got nothing to say."

She pulled a gun from her pocket and stood, feet apart, a whiskey bottle dangling from one hand and a gun from the other."

"Permission to shoot," Pearce asked Smith.

"Wait. I'll try to talk her down."

"Careful," he said.

As a wobbly Anna Wilson stood on the porch, Little Billy walked out of the house, came up from behind her, and took the gun from her hand."

"I'm the one you want," said Billy. "I killed Mattie and shot Jim. I tried to frame my mother as payback."

"You're crazy as a bed bug," said Mrs. Wilson, turning to face the cops.

"I'm the killer," she insisted.

The cops looked from one to the other, their guns swinging back and forth.

Billy threw the gun on the lawn and wrapped his arms around his mother.

"You're a mean and hateful person. You blame me for Brian's death and have punished me every day since he died. It wasn't my fault. Still, I can't let you die. You're my mother."

He let go, and Anna Wilson slid down the front wall, onto the porch, of her house.

"I'm sorry, Billy. I know you didn't mean for Brian to get hurt. I should have looked after him. I was too busy dating or working to give you boys the advice a mother should give.

"Forgive me, son. I'm so sorry."

"I love you, Mom. I forgive you."

The armed officers surrounded Billy and Mrs. Wilson, handcuffed them, and put them in the back of a patrol car.

"Which one is the killer?" Pearce said.

"We'll know when the fingerprints come back," she said. "In the meantime, I'm locking up both of them."

32

Jenny Morrison had kept her vigil for Jim Briggs, sitting by his bedside for days, hoping for a change —the slightest movement of his hand, a twitch of his eyelids.

Then it happened. Jim Briggs's eyes popped open.

"Hey, Babe, what's going on."

"You're awake."

Tears flowed down Jenny's face.

"Why are you crying?"

"I'm just glad to see you."

"I was talking to Bobbie Worth and was heading home to talk. That was an hour ago."

He had been looking at Jenny and hadn't yet registered his surroundings.

"Where am I?"

"In the hospital."

"He looked from arm to arm, wires protruding, machines beeping.

"What happened? Why am I here?"

"Someone shot you."

A bewildered look closed his face. He cocked his head.

"An unidentified person shot you in the chest. You fell and hit your head, cracking your skull and gashing your ear."

"Why am I alive if I was shot in the chest?"

"You forgot to remove your stethoscope after examining Bobbie's dog, Pepper. The stethoscope reduced the bullet's impact, which lodged in your chest muscle. Doctors removed it and patched you up. They had to drill a little hole in your thick skull to relieve the pressure from the brain bleed."

Briggs reached up and felt the bandage on his head.

"When can I get out of here?"

"Waking up from the coma doctors induced is the first step. Probably a day or two."

"Did they get the guy who shot me?"

"No, but Detective Smith has arrested two possible suspects."

"Who?"

"Little Billy Wilson and his mother, Anna."

"They conspired to kill Mattie, and then one of them shot me?"

Detective Smith says the forensic team is examining evidence from Mattie's murder to see if they can zero in on the killer. Billy claims he did it. His mother says she did. It's a long story."

"I need to sleep," he said. Briggs closed his eyes and was gone.

Jenny buzzed his nurse.

"We talked, and he asked me questions about what happened."

"Great. I'll alert the doctor."

A half-hour later, neurosurgeon Robert Edson appeared.

"I understand our patient is awake."

"He was awake, asking questions about where he was and how he got there. He had no memory of the incident."

"That he was so alert and inquisitive is a good sign," said Dr. Edson. "The loss of memory is less concerning. It's not unusual for a trauma victim to block a bad memory. As pictures of the shooting come back, he'll be upset. Therapy to deal with flashbacks and how he processes them will be critical to his recovery."

"He wants to know when he can go home."

The doctor laughed. "A common question. It's like they're screaming, 'Get me outta here,' and no one is listening. We'll work to keep him awake longer so we can graduate him to a normal sleep cycle. Getting him out of bed and walking, with support from physical therapy, will move him out of here in a week or less."

"My patients are easier. When they are ready to get up and go, we let them run."

"I didn't know you were a doctor."

"I'm not an M.D. I'm D.V.M."

"A vet?"

"Both Jim and me. We're surgeons at the Paws Care Emergency Hospital."

"I believe one of my dogs was a patient. We've got two Yorkies. The younger one, Crackles, had a liver infection treated at Paws Care."

"How can I forget," said Jenny. "Your other dog is Snap."

"Snap is Crackles pop," they said in unison and giggled.

"That was five years ago," said Edson, recovering his composure.

"Come on, how could I forget a name like that."

"Both dogs have continued to do well. Thanks to your

good doctoring. I promise to get Jim back on his feet like you did Crackles."

"I hope not," she said, straight-faced. "He'd be crawling on all fours."

They both cracked up.

After Dr. Edson left, Jenny called Rob Merritt, reported Jim's progress, and gave him an update on the police investigation.

"Good news," said Rob.

"Thanks to you and your private detective, we prevented Billy from fleeing to Mexico."

"Glad to help."

"Jenny," he said. "Remember, I can arrange to move your parents in a private medical transport to Portland where you and Jim can be together while you care for your family. I can find the best doctors."

"Rob, my mother has suddenly started to decline mentally and physically. No doubt, the stress over Dad's failing health hasn't helped. I want to stay here out of deference to my two sisters, who can't move. They need to say their goodbyes at the right time. Dad could be gone in weeks or linger for months. There is no way to predict."

"I understand," said Rob. "If things change, don't hesitate to call. And please keep me updated on Jim's progress.

33

Two weeks after Briggs suffered a gunshot and brain bleed, he was out of the hospital, riding with Jenny on his way to an interview with police.

The stitches used to close the ear gash during his fall were dissolving. Hair was growing back over the hole drilled to release the pressure on his brain.

Briggs and Jenny agreed marriage, children, and a future together could wait. They both wanted that to happen but agreed that moving her parents from Chicago—where they had lived for 60 years—and away from her sisters would be bad for everyone.

Jenny knew her sisters weren't equipped to deal with the medical issues her parents faced. Mom appeared to need memory care. Dad was about to enter hospice.

Jenny pulled her car into the visitor lot at the Chicago Police Department. They had a 10 a.m. appointment with Detective Smith, who agreed to reveal who she had arrested for shooting Jim and murdering Mattie Powell.

Smith said she and Detective Morton had squeezed a confession out of the killer.

After clearing security, an officer took Briggs and Jenny to the detective bureau and put them in a conference room.

Smith walked in a few minutes later and offered them coffee.

"Coffee with cream," said Briggs.

"Black for me," said Jenny.

Once settled, Smith opened a folder, scanned the top page, and closed it.

"This is a bizarre case with two suspects confessing. As it turns out, only one was guilty."

"So, Billy Wilson and his mother, Anna, each confessed. Mrs. Wilson's fingerprints were on the knife used to kill Mattie Powell. Forensics found both of their prints on the gun the assailant used to shoot you, Dr. Briggs."

After a little old-fashioned shoe leather and computers, we discovered that Anna Wilson had recently purchased bullets for her gun, had practiced at a shooting range, and bought a dark hoodie and sweatpants as part of a disguise."

"I remember a dark image coming out of the fog, but that's all," said Briggs.

"Memory loss is normal," said Detective Smith. Briggs and Jenny nodded.

"After we presented the evidence to Billy, he admitted that despite a lifetime suffering from his mother's insults, he felt sorry for her and didn't want her to suffer in jail the last years of her life."

"Mrs. Wilson initially tried to blame Billy, saying she wanted him dead, like her son, Brian. The trauma of what she did to frame him must have stirred her conscience. She finally told Billy it wasn't his fault that his little brother died riding his bicycle in front of a car. She admitted that she had blamed herself but took it out on Billy. As a result, the one incident cascaded into a lifetime of pain for both."

"Why kill Mattie Powell?"

"Mrs. Wilson said she knew Billy was depressed and wanted to die. Still angry at him, she confronted Mattie and urged her to reconsider. Mattie refused, telling her that she and Billy needed mental health counseling. Mrs. Wilson lost it, pulled out her knife, and stabbed Mattie repeatedly."

"Why did she leave the knife behind?"

"All she said was cutting meat had her whole life, and she wanted nothing more to do with it."

"What happens to her now?" said Briggs.

She'll go to an alcohol rehab unit at a psychiatric hospital. The D.A. will recommend charges following treatment and an evaluation of her mental condition."

"How about Billy?" said Jenny.

'Let's both find out. He asked me if he could come here today and meet with you. He has something to say. Is that okay?"

Briggs and Jenny looked at each other and nodded.

After a few minutes, Detective Smith came in, with Billy following her.

Billy sat down and said, "Dr. Briggs, I know now that you were looking after my best interest by not allowing me to die. Thank you for that. I also want to apologize for what my mother did. There's no way to make it up to you except to say I'm sorry."

Briggs looked at Detective Smith. The angel of mercy was about to be arrested for murder, tried, and jailed for the rest of his life.

"Billy, I forgive you. Now, you need to forgive yourself. Get on with your life. Make it the best it can be. I gave you a reprieve; use it wisely."

"Billy, what's next for you?" said Smith.

"My girlfriend and I are engaged. We're moving into my

mother's house, where I grew up. We'll fix it up and make it our own. Rebecca has a job in a nursery. I've got a job in a clothing store. We're even talking about kids."

"Good for you. Good luck."

Billy shook hands with Smith, Briggs, and Jenny and left the room.

Detective Smith looked at Briggs and said, "The real-life, murdering angel of mercy right in my conference room. What do you have to say for yourself?"

"Billy's statement, it's all hearsay."

"You sound like a lawyer practicing his defense."

"I'm no angel of mercy. Just a veterinarian doctoring the dogs of the homeless for free as a community service. Occasionally, I give them a vitamin shot or vaccine allowed under my paramedic license."

"I thought that might be your answer. You should know that I've looked into claims that this angel of mercy person may have killed up to a dozen people. Unfortunately, our coroner didn't perform autopsies on the Lazy Acre victims of barbiturate overdoses. She said the presence of the drug could be a drug addict's miscalculation or their desperate effort to escape homelessness."

"That sounds about right," said Briggs.

"Except, the doctor did perform one autopsy. The test turned up traces of propofol in the man's bloodstream. Isn't that a drug you carry in your black bag?"

"Of course," said Briggs. "Sadly, both at Lazy Acres and at our emergency hospital, we frequently have to euthanize sick or mortally injured animals."

"Detective Smith, you know that Propofol is commonly used in human surgeries to anesthetize patients?" said Jenny.

"That's what the coroner told me. I asked her to investigate the case to determine if the victim had been hospitalized for surgery."

Briggs and Jenny looked at her, waiting for the punch line: 'You're under arrest for murder.'

"Turns out the dead man had been treated for kidney stones. They gave him propofol, performed the procedure, and wrote him a painkiller prescription. Two hours after his release from the surgery center, he died of an overdose.

Briggs let out a visible sign of relief. When he heard the name, he realized the man wasn't one of those who had asked him to die.

"Glad you're not that angel of mercy fellow," she said.

Smith and Briggs looked into each other's eyes, unblinking. She nodded and smiled. Briggs knew who he was and what he had done. She was giving him a pass.

Smith stood up.

"Good luck in your new life in Portland," said Smith. "I hear it's a pretty place."

A WEEK LATER, Jim Briggs was back in Portland, launching his new mobile canine care business, *Have Paws—Will Travel*. Jenny continued working at Paws Care and managing the care of her parents.

He and Jenny talked often at first, but then their jobs and the burdens of her caring for her parents made it difficult to find time. Long talks became short texts.

Not long after launching the business in Portland, Briggs met police officer Kim Jansen. His life would never be the same.

ABOUT THE AUTHOR

Bruce Lewis was a crime reporter for several California daily newspapers, covering police and fire. His reporting earned six awards for best news and feature writing. He is the author of the Master Detective cover story *Bloody Murder in Beautiful Downtown Burbank*. His work as a public relations consultant earned over 30 professional awards. He lives with his wife in the San Francisco East Bay.

His books are set in Portland, Oregon, where he lived for six years (2015-2021).

He is the author of four novels: *Angel of Mercy*, *Human Strays*, *Family Curse,* and *The Red Flock*.

ALSO BY BRUCE LEWIS

Angel of Mercy is Book 1 in *The Angel of Mercy Series*. Each book is a stand-alone story with many of the same characters, including Angel of Mercy Jim Briggs.

The series, in order:

Angel of Mercy - Book 1

Human Strays - Book 2

Family Curse - Book 3

The Red Flock - Book 4

Bless Me Father—For You Have Sinned - Book 5

Thank you for reading my books.

—Bruce Lewis

Made in the USA
Middletown, DE
08 March 2024